" 'Would you tell me, pl⟨ease, which way I ought to⟩
go from here?'

'That depends a good d⟨eal on where you want to⟩
go to,' said the Cat.

'I don't much care where…' said Alice.

'Then it doesn't matter which way you go,' said
the Cat.

'…so long as I get somewhere,' Alice added as an
explanation.

'Oh, you're sure to do that,' said the Cat, 'if you
only walk long enough.' "

~ Lewis Carroll, *Alice's Adventures in Wonderland*

Praise for *IF YOU WALK LONG ENOUGH*

"Hartney's novel expresses beautifully the reality of veterans returning home from Vietnam to a world that had not stood still while they were gone. They've changed, but their worlds also changed, and everyone now has to determine if their personal piece still fits into the puzzle. A story of people you'll care about."

~Bill McCloud, Flight Operations Coordinator, 147th Assault Support Helicopter Company, author

~*~

"Nancy writes sensitively and powerfully about the aftereffects on both the veteran and those who love him. As with all wars, the pain is not over when the peace treaty is signed..."

~Dan Baxter, M.D., author, Armed Forces Radio Vietnam veteran

If You Walk Long Enough

by

Nancy Hartney

If You Walk Long Enough

Contact Information: info@thewildrosepress.com

Cover Art by *Kim Mendoza*

The Wild Rose Press, Inc.
PO Box 708
Adams Basin, NY 14410-0708
Visit us at www.thewildrosepress.com

Publishing History
First Edition, 2021
Trade Paperback ISBN 978-1-5092-3462-2
Digital ISBN 978-1-5092-3463-9

Published in the United States of America

Dedication

To Robert K. Almand,
my paternal cousin (June 30, 1942—May 13, 2017),
who spoke of his Vietnam experience
with pride and sorrow.

He served two volunteer tours in the U.S. Army Special Forces Green Berets, 1962-1969. Discharged at the rank of Staff Sergeant (P), he earned two Purple Hearts, two Bronze Star Medals, and one Silver Star. A "greenie," he came home and built a life as state park ranger, nurseryman, stepfather, and husband. As with many men of his era, Vietnam represented a defining life hallmark. Each warrior returned on a different path and, once home, realized himself and circumstances deeply changed.

Acknowledgements

Special acknowledgement to my beta readers who gave critical comments and a red pen: Pam Jones Foster, a fine author and friend, and by extension her late husband Jack Jones, Vietnam veteran; Dr. Dan Baxter and his memories of Vietnam; and regional author Jack Cotner. Thanks to poet and teacher Bill McCloud, flight operations coordinator with the 147th Assault Support Helicopter Company, for his critical eye and generous gift of time. I am grateful to Barbara Youree who shared memories of her love, lost in a PTSD morass. Each person brought something unique to the endeavor and I am indebted for their personal reflections.

Deep appreciation to several Arkansas critique groups—collectively and individually—that have nudged me forward with their comments and challenges: The Writers Guild of Arkansas (Rogers/Fayetteville), Dickson Street Writers (Fayetteville), and the Ozark Mountain Writer's Guild (Fayetteville).

Thanks to Pat Carr, fellow writer and briefly writing coach, who gave me critical revisions, friendship, and scribe tools. I appreciate her insight at a time when her days were laced with health issues. A role model on many levels.

Gratitude to my husband Bob Hartney, my brother-in-law and veteran Michael Hartney, the readers of my previously published story collections, and my personal friends for unfailing encouragement and support.

Chapter 1
Flight Out of Vietnam

March 1970

Reid stepped into the troop transport, navigated around the feet and gear of fellow soldiers, located a seat, and slumped down. He sat too heavy and uncoordinated to move, a man drugged by living, looking in opposite directions at the same time. His face crumpled as he stared at a head on the road. A leg sticking mud-deep in a rice paddy. The silence after an explosion. Thoughts of men returning in black bags. The smell of rotting vegetation.

He wiped his hand across his face and blinked until his eyes refocused. A trickle of cold sweat slid down his spine, the wet leached away by his shirt. He scratched at his chest as if scraping off a fungus.

The plane lumbered down the runway, shuddered, and lifted. A collective cheer burst from the throats of the men as the giant curved above Tan Son Nhut runway, the U.S. air base near Saigon, flying west. Out of Vietnam.

Some soldiers fell to joking with each other. A few immediately collapsed into a restless sleep. Others sat lost, personal narratives etched too deep in their faces.

"Goddamn Charlie *and* the brass!"

"Hey, baby, next stop—'The World.'"

"Holy Christ. I'm still alive and going home."

"Can you believe it? A do-over courtesy of the United States Marines."

Reid sank back in his seat, closed his eyes, and listened to the cacophony, his mind vibrating in the aftermath of two tours spanning three years in Nam away from the tobacco farm.

With his tours completed, he rotated out as an individual, bound to the other men by their warrior ethos. With a part of himself, he sought denial for things seen and done, kept whispering, *just get home. Disappear into the farm, into the tobacco.*

His flight from Saigon to Okinawa, on to California, and finally Beaufort, South Carolina, spun out in agonizing stages. He had chosen to come home slow. At each stop, men splintered off in different directions, intent on picking up the frayed threads of life, all the while leaving scraps of themselves tangled, trembling in the wind.

At the airports, he laid over a day, sometimes more, sat alone in a bar and drank, watched TV news, frowned, and allowed his eyes to dart over the people. *Cambodia? When did we bomb that country?*

From Okinawa, his second day in the terminal he called South Carolina. "Eleanor, it's me. I'm on the way back."

"I'll be waiting." Her voice carried a high, sweet note.

"No. Don't wait. No pick-up."

"No? What do you mean 'no'?"

"I'm not sure when I'll get there. I'm coming slow."

"Why?"

"I need time. Everything's falling apart. Nothing makes any sense. It's all lost. Maybe us too."

Silent, he gripped the phone until the strain numbed his hand, fumbled a moment, and replaced the receiver. Color gradually seeped back into his knuckles. He picked up his duffle as easily as if it had been a lunch sack and watched travelers scurry across the concourse. He hesitated a moment, naked without his rifle, and stepped into the human river.

The flight had landed in the California Bay Area during the small dark hours. Shuffled to a processing center, he'd been advised some were hostile to returning military men and he should consider wearing civilian clothes. A way to sidestep harassment.

"Hell, it ain't even an issue. I don't have any civvies. Besides, after Nam, I can handle a bunch of draft dodgers."

Reid walked down the corridor in uniform and glared at anyone that dared meet his eye. He stalked as close to the walls as possible, pausing before each bend or new set of stairs, as if walking point in a hostile environment. Except without protection, without a rifle. Most people made no eye contact. Others appeared startled and quickly brushed by.

Deliberately, he spent two days in the welcome lounge and then lost another day brooding among the bars, his face tense and dark. From the terminal, he considered the distant maze of lights scattered along the horizon and vaguely reflected on the unknown people living there.

Nights, best for his travel, left him exhausted and drained despite the reduced rush with fewer people. His lips pressed together in a hard line, gave him a ghoul-angry face.

On Thursday, he hopped another flight, one leg closer to that place once called home. At a news kiosk, headlines screamed at him: Nam troop levels increased, draft cards burned, civil demonstrations and riots exploding in major cities.

Reid bought a newspaper, strode to a bar, and read while sipping whiskey with a beer back. This world, different from the one he left, writhed in agony and political upheaval.

In Chicago, his warrior's sense of belonging slowly disintegrated as one-by-one, men splintered off and went their separate ways. Alone, he was simply another anonymous uniform.

He rented a locker, stuffed his duffle inside, and caught a taxi already queued for the morning passenger rush.

"Where to, soldier?"

"Navy Pier."

He wandered Lake Shore Drive, and the marina at Chicago Harbor. Gulls reeled overhead and squawked, demanded handouts, left white smears on the pilings. Boat captains stared at him, frowning as to why he would wander in the fog among their yachts. By late morning, families of tourists materialized, conferred over city maps, and wandered off to Shedd Aquarium or down to the new McCormick Center.

Reid roamed the pier and the breakwater, rode the El, stared at billboards along the trainway, and glimpsed people through the windows of their shoddy apartments. Riding was cheaper than spending the night in a flophouse and better than the airport floor. He dozed, the El's rhythm lulling him. He woke and stared out the window at winos, hookers, and partygoers milling on street corners wet with drizzle, seeing the juxtaposition of glitter and grime, windy city and hog butcher, ghetto and metropolis.

Chapter 2
Morning Phone Call

March 1970

The jangle of the phone shattered that still hour before dawn, when the world holds its breath, and waits for a new day. Ellie knew who it was before she even answered, recognized it in the prickle of her skin.

She scrambled through the sheets and across the bed, pushed the cat aside. A third ring and fourth before she could pick-up.

"Hello? Hello, Reid?"

Silence hummed on the open line.

"Reid?" She held the phone with both hands against her ear so hard it hurt, tried to squeeze sound from the cold object.

"Hello, Reid? Please answer." She gritted her teeth and sucked in her breath.

"Eleanor, it's me."

"Where are you?"

Again, a silence.

Slower, she repeated, "Reid. Where are you?" and slumped to the floor, legs curled beneath her body, and the sheet crumpled around her. The bitter taste of dread rose in her mouth. She pressed the phone closer to her ear and strained to hear.

Resonating from a distance, Reid's voice rattled

hoarse against the vacuous static of airport sounds.

"Chicago. Got a hop from the West Coast last night." He paused. "If I want it. Maybe I can get another hop later." He mumbled something unintelligible, and then said, "Maybe catch something else out from here. Can't say when... probably tomorrow night. Maybe next week... maybe longer. I might go some other place. I can't think..." His voice grew indistinct.

"Come home, Reid. I need to touch you again. Smell you. Taste you. Make sure you're not a ghost."

His voice vibrated with a remote quality. "The road's the best. Especially if you don't have a place."

"But you have a place. This is your home," she said. "Please come. I'm here. Waiting. I'll pick you up whenever you say. Doesn't matter the time."

"No, Eleanor. No pick-up." He paused, took a raspy breath, and continued. "I have to sort things out."

"What things? Tell me."

"Things. Everything needs sorting. Gotta put pieces back together."

Her temples throbbed. Her mouth filled with cotton and a stab of fear rose in her stomach. "Let's do it together. We both have things that need sorting. Please."

She flinched at a half-choking cough, the sound of a dropped receiver, and the high hum of a deadline.

She held the phone in her hands, pulled the sheet around her, and bawled until she had dry heaves. Her ear throbbed from the pressure of listening.

He called her Eleanor, not Ellie, a signal he had withdrawn again, held her at arm's length. The voice. Reid's, but not the same. Too distant. Three years gone from home, and he had morphed into a shadow and was not really there.

Blowing her nose on the sheet, she stood, tossed it on the floor, and hung the phone up before she stumbled toward the kitchen, any chance of sleep gone.

She rummaged for a cup while the coffee perked, the aroma filling the galley-sized kitchen. She opened Rosie's cat food. A rather dainty eater, the calico licked the gravy before she took a mouthful and settled into nibbling.

Turning the burner off, Ellie allowed the coffee, her holy water, to sit a minute before she poured a cup. She opened the back-porch door and held it with her hip, a steaming cup in one hand and Grover's bowl of kibbles in the other. Her morning ritual of conversation with Rosie and the yellow dog, while drinking her brew, helped ease her morning into day.

The porch, sagging from the years, offered a convenient site to survey the yard while the sun yawned awake. Blue jays nattered around the bird feeder, keeping the smaller finches and sparrows at bay. She made a mental note to refill the feeder and put out a suet block. The grass needed mowing. Maybe later in the week. For now, the country garden jumble of zinnias, tomato plants, and weeds satisfied her, plants at once challenging, competing, and balanced. Like people.

She took a shallow breath with sharp expectant edges. She could no longer picture him. Nor smell his essence. Forgiving Reid those days before he shipped, when he withdrew into himself, struggled against his father, and ignored his sister Angela, made Ellie cringe. He had done little to acknowledge their relationship those last days.

Reid was the only man who had ever made love to her in the rain. They sat at a picnic table and drank wine before a summer squall moved across the county. The rain mirrored their ache and fervor—the sunlit clouds, fat drops, hard short deluge, and, finally, a clearing, an end. Afterwards, laughing they carved their initials on the table to mark the day, April 1965.

Now, five years later, she stood before her garden, remembered those two people in their twenties, holding hands on the courthouse steps after a justice of the peace officiated marriage. Although she remembered their radiant faces, she could no longer see details. Worse, she could barely recall her feelings.

His phone call tangled her thoughts. Thomas Wolfe was wrong about going home. James Baldwin came closer to reality: Home is not a place but more like a constant condition.

She drank the last of her coffee, tossed the dregs, and went inside to dress for work. After all, tourism and the Chamber of Commerce waited on no one. Except, of course, funding sponsors.

Chapter 3
Airport Pick-up

March 1970

Late on Sunday, Reid arranged the last leg home and called his sister Angela.

"I'm landing Frogmore tomorrow. Pick me up."

"Reid, that you?"

He was not sure if she was surprised by the call or being sarcastic. Either way, he swallowed and tried to choke down the irritation rising in his throat.

"Yeah."

"Pick you up? I'm your sister. I'm family. Of course, I'll pick you up. But Ellie should pick you up. She's your wife."

"Yeah, well, not gonna happen like that. You pick me up," he repeated. "Damn girl, there never was much family. Now even that's gone."

"Is that what you think? Aren't me and Ellie both family?" Angela's voice quavered, fell, and finally shuddered across the distance.

He frowned in exasperation, watched passersby flow through, rubbed the bridge of his nose against a possible headache, and answered with a growl.

"Eleanor married in. Doesn't count. Not real family."

"She's your wife. You chose her. Can't get much

more family than that." Again, that catch in Angela's voice.

"I might have been wrong."

"What are you saying?"

"A lot has happened these last years." He leaned against the wall. Too many people rushing without purpose to nameless places. The rise and fall of conversations. An abrasive squawk of flight announcements. He put a hand over his ear and pressed the phone hard against his other ear to cut the noise. He groaned.

"Damn right it has. You've got things to answer for," Angela said, her voice cracking again.

"Pick me up." His jaw muscle tightened. He glared at people standing too close.

"Beaufort is a long way from here," she said. "I'll lose most of a day by the time I drive over, get through the snarl of airport, pick you up, and get back home."

"So what? You don't have a day for your brother? What about the days I lost? Pick me up." He banged the receiver into its cradle, stood tense on the Delta concourse, and watched the ebb and flow of planes and people. All things moved. Nothing stood still. He needed a shower and clean clothes.

Chapter 4
Frogmore Airport

March 1970

When the jet set down at the South Carolina's Frogmore airport, Reid hung back until his fellow passengers disembarked and the cleaning crew started down the aisle. He got off last, not trusting that his sister would pick him up. He stopped at the end of the walkway tunnel before stepping into the arrival area and scanning for her.

Angela stood on the concourse in a plaid dress, her face sun-browned, and waved. Despite the lack of a crowd, she held her arm high, and signaled him.

He hesitated. She slowly dropped her arm, then stood again on tiptoe, smiled, and waved at him.

Relief spread across his face. He returned her smile and moved in her direction.

She peered at him from behind coke-bottle thick glasses, grabbed him, and hugged with the solid strength of a farm hand. He partially relaxed against her firm shape, square hands, and country presence. A fragile reassurance emanated from her.

"Little brother. You're thin as a fence rail. Downright skinny. Didn't like the food there?" She held him at arm's length, eyed him up and down, and wrapped him in her arms again.

"Not that, Big Sis. Too many parties," he said, his face rumpling into a road map of lines. "Uncle Sugar's finest resort on the South China Sea. Free flowing beer. Horny army nurses. Exotic smokes. Sweet hell, it was party, party, party. Why eat and ruin the buzz?"

"Must have been some party judging from the lack of letters," she said.

"Don't start on the goddamn letters," he growled and headed for the baggage claim area.

"Now that you are away from the excitement, we'll get you fattened up. Then we have serious talking to do." She pulled him into another hug and kissed him on the cheek. "I'm glad you're home."

"I'll take the fattening-up but put a hold on the rest of that shit." He threw the words over his shoulder, retrieved a gray-green duffle from the carousel, and bent down to check the tag.

"That all the stuff you have?" she asked.

"Yeah. This is it." He tapped the lumpy sack with his boot. "I'm learning to shed stuff, travel light."

"You've never been a *GQ* fashion plate. Nor a pack rat. You were ugly before you left, but now, even gnawed shoe leather has more sex appeal." Angela began weaving her way toward the terminal exit.

He hoisted the duffle to his shoulder. Exit doors glided open and a moist coating settled on arms, hands, and faces, the benefits of air conditioning. They flowed out of the congested terminal into the sodden summer.

He glanced sideways at Angela's plain appearance, near-sighted squint, and clunky shoes with the cotton dress. He smiled. She had dressed up for him, and he realized he was happy to see her. She had faulted him, held on to old grievances, but never mind, they were still family, still Holcombe. Three years was a long time.

"First thing I need is Leroy's," he said as they crossed the maze of sidewalks and one lane turnouts. "A cold beer with a plate of fried catfish with cheese grits."

"Still the best greasy spoon in the county. You buy," she said. "But be prepared to hit the fields once we get home."

"You mean you need help getting that tobacco in?" He shook his head and grinned. "I thought Reynolds and Phillip Morris—the big boys—sent fellers out to pick for you while we were fighting communism, making the world safe for democracy. Building markets for Coca-Cola and Marlboros."

Angela snorted. "Those boys sit in air-conditioned offices and haul in the money from us dirt farmers."

"Hell. Might've known. It's not me you want. It's the stoop work you're after."

"You got it." She play-punched him on the arm.

"No problem, Sis. Be happy to help you get rich off my sweat." He glanced at her hands—short nails, work cracked skin, finger joints knotting.

"I'm sure not getting wealthy. But you know what? Maybe if you work hard enough, the bank loan officer will send you a personal, handwritten, thank you note." She cackled and kept walking.

He laughed. "I see you still got a sense of humor."

Humidity radiated up from the asphalt in filmy images and heat penetrated their shoe soles as they tramped across the parking area to Lot C and a faded pickup in the last row.

"I'll be tarred and feathered. You still got Jim

14

Guy's Chevy. Looks good for a '55." Reid slung his gear into the pick-up bed. "Helluva fine truck, dents and all."

As teens, they had driven countless miles over washboard roads drinking beer, cussing each other, dreading the work, and relishing being outside. They were each ever ready to pull a prank.

"Never did fix that hail damage." He gestured at the dinged hood.

"Nope. No sense fixing ugly. Burns a little oil, but she's good. Paid for. Like Jim Guy used to say, 'Not broke. Leave it be.'"

He jerked at the passenger door several times before he could wrench it open.

"Welcome home." Angela hooted and ran her hand across the cracked vinyl seat. "You asked for a ride. This's the only limo I got at the farm."

"Sweet hell. Get the damn door fixed."

"You got in. What's the complaint?" She threw the Chevy in reverse, shifted to first, and navigated past the tollbooth.

Reid rolled the window down and draped his hand out, allowing it to bounce on the wind. Traffic hummed as they picked up speed, drove north out toward Willington, their hometown in the heart of tobacco country.

Except for the addition of a neon sign near the Lake Moultrie turnoff, Leroy's Prime Eats stood exactly as he remembered; set back from the road, crouched in a grove of live oaks, its warped siding bleached colorless. The gravel parking lot glistened with stagnant puddles.

Inside, wobbly tables with red-and-white

checkered plastic coverings and mismatched chairs accommodated customers. Odors of fried chicken, hickory smoked ribs, too-hot cooking lard, and fresh-baked biscuits mingled in the restaurant haze. The windows, cloudy with grunge, allowed a thin light inside while the air conditioner wheezed and coughed, struggling against the mugginess.

At two o'clock, most of the noon crowd had finished lunch and left. A broad-hipped cashier signaled them to sit wherever they wanted.

Angela picked a table and scraped a straight-backed chair across the linoleum. Reid took off his service jacket, draped it on a chair, and loosened his tie. They ordered draft beers.

"How does it feel?"

"What?"

She held her hands open in a broad gesture. "Being back."

He flashed a crooked smile and licked foam off his lips. "Good being back in the Palmetto State. Good drinking *cold* beer." He held his mug to the light, admired the liquid amber, and took a long swallow, Adam's apple bobbing.

"That's it?"

"What else?" He shrugged. "Okay. I feel okay."

"Just okay? Three years gone and just okay?" She propped her elbows on the table, hands still open, and stared at him.

"Different. Good. Bad." He did not have words for the confusion of his feelings, for the losses, for the regrets.

A pear-shaped waitress sashayed up, sat sweating water glasses on the table, and took their order. A few minutes later, she placed plates heaped with fried catfish, cole slaw, hushpuppies, and green tomato pickles on the table. "Bring you anything else?" She popped her gum, stuck a pencil behind her ear, and tucked the order pad in an apron pocket.

They shook their heads "no" and began eating without further talk. There was comfort together without needing words. The Old Man had always pushed them to eat and get back to work, not carry on a conversation.

Finished, they shoved their plates aside.

"What are you going to do?" she said.

"Whatever I damn well please." He lit a cigarette, took a deep drag, and exhaled slow, tilting his head to blow smoke up. He stared down at the Zippo, a favorite among soldiers, even those that did not smoke, and clicked it closed. His face indecipherable, a roadmap littered with lines and dark stubble.

"Hell, I might get ambitious and go back to college. My favorite uncle will pay for it. Make something of my life now that I've been spared," he said.

"Tobacco starts in another month. I need you every day with fieldwork. We still have to handle other farm matters. Whatever you plan better happen fast." Angela leaned back and crossed her arms.

"I know. I gotta set my part of the world upright again. It takes time."

"You've got personal things to get right too." She uncrossed her arms and leaned forward, propping elbows on the table.

"Like what?"

"Don't be a wise-ass. Your wife Ellie? How about

me? What to do with the farm?"

"You mean Eleanor?" He rubbed a grease spot on the plastic tablecloth and flicked at a fly. "She wrote. Regular. Sent a few snapshots. I called on my way back. Told her not to pick me up." He tapped the ash off his cigarette.

"Why did you do that?" The chair creaked as Angela shifted. "She's your wife and you need to be at her place. Pick up your husbandly duties." She arched an eyebrow and flashed a wicked smile.

"I still have a hard-on for her." He snorted, blew smoke up, and watched it disappear.

"What does that mean?" She leaned back and glared at him.

"Don't know." He took another deep drag, held it, and blew out in a long stream.

"So, what are you going to do?"

He sat silent, and then spoke in a low voice. "Not sure. We're still legal." He watched the ash on his cigarette lengthen, bend, and collapse into the ashtray.

"This makes no sense." Angela wadded her napkin and stuffed it next to her plate. "She's your wife and you tell her to stay away. You say you have a thing for her. Do you love her? Or just need the punch? What the hell are you thinking?"

Reid chugged the last of his Bud and motioned to the waitress for another.

"She stayed in touch with me, despite our sister-in-law status." Angela took her glasses off and rubbed her eyes. "We have gotten pretty close. Don't know what I would have done without her. Before Jim Guy died, we had the farm in the black. Barely, but still black. He respected the land. No matter." She replaced her glasses.

"Daddy treated us like hired help. Both of us. Especially me, his own daughter. Damn that old man's soul. He ran the farm into the ground. *Deliberately.*"

Reid stared at his plate, pushed fish bones through a watery-mayonnaise pool with his fork. He kept his head down.

"When that tractor rolled on Jim Guy..." She made a low coughing sound, ran her finger up and down the sweating mug, leaving trails in the condensation, and continued. "With him gone and me alone, you not even bothering to write or come for his funeral, I was lost. Ellie stood by me. We had no idea if you were dead or alive. What the dickens?"

"Ah, Sis." Frowning, he placed a hand on her arm. "Things happened over there. Hard things. Mean things. I'm not the same. I'm *so* different. I can't explain."

She stared at his hand, laced with puckered scars and a faint discoloration around the nails. "We didn't exactly stand still either. Hard stuff happened here too. You think two funerals in one year easy?"

"You don't know funerals." He slugged back his beer, motioned for another, and saw body bags on a chopper spiraling away in dust, reflected on empty basecamp bunks, soon filled with a newbie from Alabama or Iowa, maybe California, full of questions. A scenario repeated and repeated.

He shivered, sat silent, and stared at town traffic crawling past, spewing exhaust fumes. Mid-afternoon heat shimmered in waves on the asphalt. Add an afternoon thundershower with sputtering mopeds, lumbering army trucks, a cacophony of horns, and it could be Saigon.

Angela nursed her single draw and studied his face.

By late afternoon, blue-collar workers on their way home drifted in and filled the place with rowdy jokes, cigarette smoke, and, from the back, the clunk of cue stick on pool balls.

"Let's go, little brother." She scraped the chair away from the table. "No sense hanging out here. I have an hour drive and evening chores waiting. I'll drop you at Ellie's place."

"No. Not there. Not ready for her. Not yet."

"Now where the devil do you expect to go?" She frowned, stood with her hand on the back of the chair, hip cocked sideways.

"You need me for the tobacco. I'll sleep in my old room."

She glared at him, her jaw clenched, muscles bulging. "How dare you say that to me like *you* can save everything. Jim Guy and I handled the farm until his accident. For the last year, I have been handling everything *alone*. *Everything*. Nothing from you. Zilch. Zero."

He stubbed out the cigarette. "Too much has happened to sort it out right now."

"Damn right. You didn't write. You didn't call. You didn't come for the funerals—for neither Jim Guy nor that old man. Didn't offer anything for the farm even before you shipped. It's got to be sorted sooner or later. Maybe not now or here, but soon." She stood square, glared at him, and stomped to the door.

He sat alone, smelled diesel fuel and burned bodies. Saw a village child smile at him. Heard someone pull a trigger, a short violent burst. Sweat slid down his forehead and stung his eyes. He coughed, wiped his face, stood, and tossed a handful of crumpled bills on the table. He slung the jacket over his shoulder and followed his sister.

Chapter 5
The Farm, Day One

March 1970

Reid lay in bed and listened to the silent house. Angela would be up soon to get the coffee perking in an old-fashioned pot. Probably fix pancakes and fry bacon strips—his favorites.

He rose and dressed. Pansy needed milking. The barn cats queuing up for a share of warm milk. Chickens wanting corn scratch. Those early chores he had missed while in Nam.

He slipped outside, morning dew still on the grass. The eastern sky reddened as the sun stretched awake. Bugle, the farm dog, swung into step ahead of him.

Reid focused his attention on outside chores as if he had never left. For that, he was grateful. While most things appeared the same on the outside, he nonetheless knew in his gut, nothing would *ever* be the same again.

People no longer alive. Days smothered in heat. Ghosts that floated out of reach. Spells etched on palm tree fonds. Folktales of man-monkey apparitions. Life gnawed on him.

Ellie—Eleanor—their marriage less than five years old and already stagnant despite their sweat-soaked nights, candy-laced dreams, and shared laughter. They had started out passionate, locked into each other emotionally, thinking it would last. Until insidious cracks appeared.

His father, in constant conflict with him, had been against Ellie from the first time Reid had shown interest.

Angela sided with their father, and then swung back and supported Reid, only to become hypercritical of both after their JP-officiated marriage.

Jim Guy, her husband, had remained neutral, the balancing fulcrum for the family. She railed at him as being too easygoing and forgiving and then grew silent and ashamed of her anger.

Ellie had been different from any woman Reid had known before. Not a beauty but unusual with brown eyes set a little too close, freckles, high cheekbones, and kinky, unkempt red curls. She had waltzed off to a Boston college, defying Willington town gossips' admonishments against northern liberals and race mixing. Her father, a Methodist preacher, silently supported her choice but did nothing to slow wagging tongues. After three years at Wellesley College, she transferred to Clemson University to finish her degree saying, "Darling, I'm not running back home, I'm *remaking* home."

Now he could scarcely remember what he had wanted from her or why he married. Lust mostly, but soul mates too. He quietly hunkered down on the farm and sorted through his feelings, retreating to a less troubled time. His neck ached. He rolled his shoulders and stretched to relieve the muscles. The last three years left him exhausted. Even here, on the farm, ghosts gathered, their eyes accusing. They worried him.

Some guys back from Nam, put a coin in their

mouth and kissed a train. More than one of his Southern buddies with too much guilt, took a dog, went bird hunting, and didn't come back.

He knew families and communities absorbed the loss and moved on. After all, with a flood plain for your soul, water creeps into the cracks, drowns memories, and bares hidden places to the light.

He never learned how to forgive himself or others and, in that respect, took after the old man. He tried, but never quite succeeded.

****

Angela watched Reid from the kitchen window as he came to the house from the barn. He stopped and gave the cats a splash of milk in their upturned hubcap, opened the screen door, clumped across the porch into the kitchen, and set the pail in the sink. He washed up and poured himself coffee.

She took a sip of her second cup, placed it on the laminated table, and gestured for him to fix a plate and start eating. She strained the milk.

A morning anchor to her day, she rather liked doing the milking, missed the quiet time with the cow.

With Jim Guy and her father gone, she no longer made buttermilk. They had both loved the sour taste of the fermented drink. Now she most frequently skimmed the cream for butter, saved the blue john, and clabbered the rest into cottage cheese. She gave most of it to families living on the south end of town. It made her feel useful, especially since those folks had limited resources. She reminded herself not to feel too holy giving it away, but to remember to "trade" later for summer vegetables, fall pecans, or a sack of quilting scraps.

Reid heaped pancakes on his plate and doused them in cane syrup. The liquid dripped down the sides, adding a brown ribbon to the beige stack. He slouched over his food and began eating.

"The tobacco is coming in good." Angela watched him eat. "We've had regular rain. Time to start topping and breaking suckers. I need you out there."

"I know what has to be done," he said.

"We can handle part of the field this morning before the heat gets up."

"Jesus in a raincoat, Sis, I know heat. Real crotch-rot heat. Don't tell me about tobacco. I was whelped in these fields."

The pitch of his voice, his pursed lips, and furrowed forehead screamed irritation. She held her tone steady and continued talking. "I have an appointment with Cavanagh down at the bank at two this afternoon."

"Oh yeah? Why? What's that knot-head-bloodsucking bureaucrat got to do with anything?"

The kitchen clock chimed the half hour. The orange tom sashayed toward the door as if reminded of an appointment. She rose and opened the door for him. The house settled back into silence.

Neither Reid nor Angela spoke for long minutes. Finally, she cleared her throat, fumbled a second, and shook her head.

"Me and Jim Guy handled this place these last years," she said. "Even with my teaching and working the fields during summers, it's been sinking. Daddy took a second mortgage. He hated paying on the notes so that was another problem."

"But I thought he *wanted* to take care of money

things."

"Got to where he hated the bankers, called them "Suits." Said they were leeches. Couldn't make him file taxes—something he had to do—so penalties piled up. He even had a hard time voting. Too rock headed. He went to weed his last year, seemed like a deliberate decision."

"Gotta hand it to the old devil, he understood how to grow tobacco." Reid stabbed another wedge of pancakes into his mouth. He chewed, elbows on the table, fork posed over the food. He ate fast, gobbling before the next mortar round hit.

She stared at him, then spoke again. "If the place is half yours, better set your mind on hard work and debt."

"Don't tell me hard work." He slammed his fork down. "You think those months in that hellhole country easy? You think I can't hump whatever needs doing? Tobacco's nothing. Don't preach hard to *me*."

She rose from the table and continued talking. "American and Philip Morris have an eye on all of the small farms in the county. They are buying allotments. Sometimes they simply grab the land especially if back taxes are hanging out. For the most part, folks are consolidating or becoming white sharecroppers. Make no mistake, profits are flowing. Just not into our pockets. Professional thieves with tailor-made suits out there these days."

He sagged, his head in his hands. After a few moments, he straightened, stared at her, and said, "Bet the Old Man is rolling over in his grave what with the bank trying to take this place. I say good damn riddance."

"You crazy bastard," she said. "This farm has been

in our family for three generations now. I don't intend to let it go."

Silent, he glared across the kitchen at her.

"With Jim Guy gone, I can't run this place. Not alone." She leaned on the counter, crossed her arms, and spoke low. "If you plan on staying and helping, that's different. We do it together. Otherwise, things are changing. Everything from farming to politics is moving faster than you even think."

"I never meant to live here. Don't want to be a farmer." He swirled his coffee around and noticed the roughness of his hands against the smooth cup.

"That it? You dump off farm and family on your way out of town?"

"Whoa, big Sis. Don't get your panties up your butt." He stared at her, stifled his impulse to slam the table across the room. "Family ties are never what they're cracked up to be. They create conflict and only pay off once in a while."

She picked up the coffee pot, refilled Reid's cup, her own, and sat down again. She clinked the spoon around in the brown liquid, picked up the brew and held it, appreciating the warmth. "I always figured a fifty-fifty pay off when it comes to families."

Silent, he pushed his plate away and planted his elbows on the table, a signal he wanted no more, normal in Nam but rude in polite company.

From where he sat, he could see the farm. He scrutinized the twenty-foot-tall curing barn, the tool shed's peeling roof, and the corncrib, listing right.

Beyond the pasture stretched row-crops as far as he could see. Although rooted here as a family, he realized, things had become untethered, were sliding apart—his directions, his marriage, the farm, the times. All things were dissolving into a twilight realm.

Angela broke the silence. "Daddy wanted you to have this place. When Mother left, he nearly quit. He hung on because he wanted you and him to run the farm. You know, the father-son thing."

"That why he stayed on me all the time? Belittled me. Slammed me around?" He sucked air through his teeth and shook his head, his face distorted in a frown. "I think he stayed on me, to show me and everyone else, who was big boss. He was spiteful. Mean."

"Oh, for crying out loud, Reid. It's God's own truth, Daddy never showed love for *anyone*. The man was cold, impenetrable. Mother saw that and left. If he hadn't been mean, he never could have survived. He learned from his father, who learned from his father."

Reid exhaled. "Well, sweet hell take all of it. Make no mistake, never *was*, nor *ever will be*, a father-son thing for me."

She sat her cup on the table with a distinct thud. "Careful. You're not much different. As soon as you get your legs under you, you're gone."

They fell silent, barely acknowledged each other, patterns repeated from prior decades.

"Daddy treated me and Jim Guy like field hands," Angela said. "He gave us free rent but constantly reminded us of that. Pitiful attempt to sooth his conscience. We went into *personal* debt trying to help him with planting, harvesting, and medical bills. You can thank Jim Guy for being generous. When you left for college, I could see Daddy crumble. Then you and Ellie got married and he got meaner, simply stopped trying." She sighed, her face weather-beaten from too much sun. And worry.

A farmwife and schoolteacher, with additional obligations as sister and sister-in-law. Barely post thirty, married and widowed, she was alone and lonely. She didn't know which proved more troublesome.

Reid, hands fumbling with an unlit cigarette, listened to her, and watched her shuffle around the kitchen, disorganized and distracted, before sitting down.

Angela brushed a fly off the table and spoke low. "Those big buyers came around pretty quick after Jim Guy's accident. With Daddy and Jim Guy gone, me only half owner, those boys didn't figure I could handle the place. They hoped I'd let go, default on the loan. Well, surprise. I'm still here. But not for much longer. Hang their greedy souls."

He picked up a spoon, dumped in several heaps of sugar, and stirred. "I'm not a farmer. I don't want to grow tobacco. Memories here strangle me. Especially talk and gossip from all the self-righteous bigots." He stared into the dark liquid.

"Bigots? Think you're different?"

His head snapped up. "Meaning what?" He scowled.

"Maybe you take after the old man more than you think."

He picked up his coffee, now cold, and swilled it.

"You owe me for hanging on, so you have an inheritance." She slapped the table as she rose and cleared breakfast dishes. "Keep that in mind."

"Don't get self-righteous on me. You're entitled to half the place. Work it right, I might even *give* you the whole thing. For now, I've got other things to settle."

"Now that's a *real* bargain with all the debt this place has piled up." She busied herself running dishwater. "What do you think about keeping this place, hire a farm manager? No halves." She turned the water off, and watched him.

"Manager? Like who?"

"Someone like Calvin Terrell or his son Joe." She poured herself more coffee and leaned her hip against the sink. "Terrell is a respected name, and they are hard workers. They know farming."

"Are you crazy? You know how folks feel about coloreds. Doesn't make any difference where they've been or who they are nor how long they've lived here. They're still only good for field work, sweat work."

"Don't you think I know that? Times must change. *We* have to change too. Besides, Calvin has helped me run this place and is helping me get a picking crew. He's my *de facto* manager. I've gotten mean comments from some folks around here but Calvin's the only decent farmer in our tri-county area."

He leaned forward. "I say 'No.' Not just no, but sweet hell no. Those people are hired hands only. Stoop labor. Besides, what about the debt?"

"Weren't you in Nam with him?" she asked.

He averted his head. "Who?"

"Joe. Calvin's son." She sipped her coffee and watched him through narrowed eyes.

"I think he was there same time. Never saw him." He shifted in his chair, toyed with his cup, and allowed his mind to wander.

Outside the window, the old mule and cow grazed across the pasture, a mismatched couple always near each other. Life on the land revolved around the seasons, giving structure and stability to animals and humans.

"He came home four weeks ago," Angela said. "Mary told me he got shot up a bit saving another man. Has a gimp leg now."

"Yeah, well, maybe I did run into him once in the PX. Didn't speak, sort of acknowledged each other and went on. Rules the same there as here. You stay with your own kind."

"He *is* your kind," she said.

"My kind? How you figure?"

"Southerner. Dirt farmer. Poor. Vet. Angry. Only difference, Joe's going to college this fall. He's going to make something of his survival."

"You forget what color he is?"

"I didn't forget anything. Man's still a farmer. If it hadn't been for Calvin, I couldn't have gotten a crew this year. I might add, Calvin helped when Jim Guy died, while white neighbors mostly stood around mouthing sympathy, asking could they help as they backed out the door. Calvin showed up unannounced and set to work. He knew what needed doing and he did it. He's a *good man*."

"College doesn't sound like farming to me. Where's Joe going?" Reid uncrossed his arms and sprawled back in the chair.

"Howard University. Calvin says Joe wants a degree in history or sociology. Says he wants to go into politics."

"Politics? Got some highfaluting ideas. Doesn't he realize this is the old South?"

"Don't *you* realize what's going on? Boycotts. Sit-ins. Marches. King assassinated. Kennedy killed. You may have been in a hell hole, but brother dearest, you've come home to a *real cauldron.*" She shook her head, sat her cup down. "Joe says he thinks with all the registration and voting drives, he can help make a difference. *For blacks and whites.*"

"What the hell? Make a difference. Changes don't go over down here especially when race is involved," he said.

"Guess you don't remember it was Mary and her church that housed all those rights activists that came through here on their way to Mississippi and Alabama when Joe was a kid."

Reid glared but did not respond.

"You've been gone so you don't know. People are pushing for human rights, one-step at a time. Everyone needs a break," she said. "People deserve equal treatment."

He continued to glower at her. "And you want to put him on regular wages, no halves? Where do you get off?"

"You may not know, but boys around here are burning draft cards and taking off for Canada. Community's unraveling. We used to be one town, help each other out. Now it's divided, splitting. It's gotten too polarized."

"Nothing we can do now from here." He picked up his coffee cup, stepped out, and sat on the back stoop.

****

Reid stared across the farm. He was standing in a tobacco field while part of him remained in a rice paddy a world away. South Carolina. Vietnam. Two places, different and the same. He wiped his face, remembered days given over to grass cuts and mosquitos. He lit a cigarette, and smoked it down until it scorched his fingers, and then fieldstripped the butt, dropped the crumpled wad in his pocket.

Under the fig tree, a striped cat cleaned its face. Bugle, sitting near his feet, thumped her tail, mouth stretched into a doggy grin. A thrush hopped from branch to branch before flitting away. The farm was peaceful, a lean-to shelter in an emotional rainsquall.

Angela finished washing the dishes and stepped outside, the screen door slapped closed behind. She sat on the step beside him. They barely glanced at each other, both silent and brooding.

"Tobacco prices lower than usual this year. Two missed bank payments hanging out there. Back taxes. With Daddy gone, we don't have any personal leverage," she said.

Reid sat silent. Like his old man, he struggled with feelings. He couldn't understand nor appreciate the necessary give and take of relationships. He coughed, as if a bone had caught in his throat, tried to swallow it down.

"Jim Guy was turning things around, but now, it's beginning to go wrong," Angela said. "That's why I need Calvin. His son Joe too, if he'll work the summer." She continued speaking, her voice dropping as she stared across the yard. "We either use them fairly or let debt eat the place and the bank forecloses."

Flies settled on the hubcap, dabbed around for left over milk. The striped cat, face grooming complete, picked her way across the yard, and disappeared into the barn. A breeze stirred the leaves, shifting the patterns of shadow and light.

Angela took a final swallow and cradled the coffee

cup.

Reid smoked another cigarette, then stood and stretched. "I need to drive into the base. Got some final paperwork stuff needs doing. Hand me the keys."

"No 'may I' use the truck?"

Face blank, he gestured impatiently at her.

"Why not see Ellie while you're out that way? You *are* married."

He snorted. "You mean Eleanor? We're divorced. Don't have papers, but it's the same thing."

"Do you think you should at least discuss it with her? Like a man—in person? Maybe try again before you grab ass and run?"

He did not answer.

She continued as if remembering aloud, her voice rough. "I tried to get Daddy to do right by Calvin. He wouldn't because he wanted to keep that man 'in his place'. Didn't want to squabble with white neighbors over Negros. Crazy rock-headed notions. Never would change a decision once it'd been made. You're like him."

Reid tossed the last of his coffee on the grass. "I know what *he* wanted to do with the place. What he wanted from me. Never mind what I wanted—or anyone. He's gone and will never know what happens."

"You'll know. You'll have it inside even if you never say it. Besides, you've still got your own guilt to handle."

"Guilt? About what?"

"Me. Ellie. Nam. Don't think I can't see it."

His back on her, he shoved his hands into his pockets, and gritted his teeth. "What the sweet hell with Nam?"

"I follow things. I hear what that newscaster Cronkite and the others say. Body counts. My Lai. Tét." She glanced down at her thick hands and massaged her fingers already knotted from farm work. "That stuff had to smear off on you."

"What do you know of guilt? Of anything? You've lived here safe all your life. You got no idea what went on over there."

She slowly nodded, pulled her glasses off, and folded her hands in her lap. "Yes, I've lived here all my life, except for college. I don't know what happened over there. Only know from the news. But I do know what has been going on here with the old man and Jim Guy. And Ellie losing her baby. Us sinking in debt. Race riots. Campus killings right here in South Carolina. Our home."

"What the hell you talking about? You got it wrong. Students are lining up to beat the draft. They are wimping out."

"Whoa, brother. Carolina state police killed three at Calalfin College, over in Orangeburg. Last month. That's a sister campus to State."

"That's a black college."

"Those *students* were unarmed. It's not right. Hear me good little brother, you are in a maelstrom of changes."

Silence.

"You need family. I'm your sister. Except for Ellie, I'm all you've got." A warmth rose in her face, probably turned her cheeks red.

"What makes you think I need anyone? Anything?" His face twisted with memories, eyes glaring and haunted.

She threw her hands up, stepped inside, jerked the extra truck keys off a pegboard, leaned out the door, and tossed them to Reid.

He caught them with a flick of his wrist. "I'll pick up some used wheels soon."

"You do that. Don't want you beholden to me. Or anyone."

She let the porch door slam.

Chapter 6
Midnight

March 1970

The ringing, unrelenting and rude, jarred Reid out of a troubled sleep. He stumbled into the kitchen and fumbled for the phone, caught it on the fifth ring.

A disembodied voice vibrated into Reid's ear.

I'm burning. My head's pounding. Everything's crumbling. Bodies twisting, running. And the screams. Stop the screams. Can't close my eyes. Can't sleep.

"Man, you need to hold on," Reid said. "You can't quit now. You're home. You're back in The World. We survived. Didn't come all this distance to throw it away."

I see them. The voice rose in panic, and then crashed with a strangled gurgling. *I see them.*

The muscles in Reid's arm jerked. He shivered and stared at a nebulous form in the corner slightly out of reach.

You should have left me.

"For chrissake, I couldn't."

We agreed—either one got bucked up, the other would help. You should have got me a tits-up bag.

"I couldn't do it. No black bag. Couldn't be sure how bad things would be. Sometimes docs fix stuff." His hands shook. Sweat beaded on his forehead.

My favorite señorita and me coiling up in smoke spirals. How cool is that? Free, you know?

Tears and mucus dripped onto Reid's chest. "How could I know?"

The voice, this time pitched low, *I'll always see those rice paddies. Those people. The killing. The stink. The taste. The waste.*

"I couldn't leave you."

Here no one sees. They're all deaf. No one understands.

"We're home."

Sleazy politicians. Card burners. All the brass yellow cowards. The voice climbed an octave.

"Hang in. We're not quitters. We do our duty. We follow orders. Tell me okay. Tell me you'll try." Reid gripped the phone until his knuckles lost color.

Silence.

"Tell me you're not going to cut and run." Reid wiped his hand across his nose, smeared snot. "No ferryman. No River Styx. Say okay."

Stillness, then finally, barely audible, a choked, *Okay.*

Reid bent forward, rested his head against the wall, hand relaxing, and the buzz slowing. He straightened as if moving through mud.

Angela stood in the doorway, silent, her face haggard, eyes questioning.

Chapter 7
Phone Natter

March 1970

As soon as she got to the Chamber of Commerce office Monday, Ellie dialed the radio to pop music, switched the light on, and made coffee. The ritualistic arrangement of Styrofoam cups, spoons, sugar packets, and creamer for office visitors, formed an anchor to her day, before the hubbub arrived.

From her work alcove opposite the rack with tourist brochures, she could see the entrance, curved information desk, and short hall leading to the conference room across from the director's office. A glass wall facing the sidewalk offered a view of ornamental trees, parking meters, and passers-by, a window on the world. At least, part of the world. She poured herself a cup of fresh coffee.

Standing at the end of the counter, she sipped the hot liquid, and began sorting through the mark-up flyer proofs when the phone rang. She answered. Ellie recognized Angela's voice vibrating with frustration.

"Reid's home. I picked him up yesterday."

"He called me and said *not* to pick him up, wouldn't say when he was coming in. Damn him." Ellie twisted the phone cord around her hand, took a deep breath, and released the cord. "Is he injured? Missing a leg or hand or anything? I don't think he could cope with that." She took another breath, her heart racing, and lowered her voice to a whisper. "Truth is, neither can I."

Angela sighed. "No, honey, bless his heart. That son-of-a-rascal just acts distracted and distant. Got puckered scars on his hands, up his arms. Looks like he hasn't slept in weeks. Lost weight."

"Where's he staying?"

"Here. At the farm. In his old bedroom. I'm not sure how I feel with him here. In fact, I'm not sure how I feel about a lot of things these days."

"He should come home, to me." Ellie shuffled the proofs across her desk. Irritation spiked up her neck and spread across her shoulders. She rotated her head and changed hands on the phone to relieve the tension.

"Yes, I know. I told him that very thing. I don't know what he's thinking, or why he's doing this." Angela sighed and continued, her voice sounding tired. "With tobacco gearing up and the farm bank note in arrears, I don't have the strength to fight with him."

Ellie gritted her teeth and vaguely shook her head. "He doesn't want to see me? Does he even ask?" She glanced at her reflection in the window, noted the dark circles under her eyes, the grim set to her mouth, and the uncontrolled mass of red curls. She had never considered herself a beauty. But now, at twenty-five, exhausted, she gritted her teeth and rebalanced her thoughts. "At least he's here, not lost in some motel or wandering around an airport."

"I resent him dumping on me," Angela said. "Leaving the farm, not coming to the funerals, and ignoring all the debt. Lately, I've accumulated a full library of resentment."

"Stop it. Stop and remember not everything's bad. There are good memories too."

Silence quivered along the line, then Angela cleared her throat and said, "You're right. Not everything's bad. I've got good memories, too. But they are so fragile. The good memories almost drown in all the changes that keep happening. It's a mixed bag. I'm wrung out."

They fell silent again.

Finally, Angela said, "I'm guessing he'll stay through the final picking and auction, then light out. The devil can chew on whatever's leftover."

"Oh, Angela, damn everything, Jim Guy's accident, your dad's death, running the farm alone... it all came too fast for me. Add Reid's reticence to the mix and...I need him with me..." Ellie's voice dissolved.

"Oh, rot. I need him too. Need help with tobacco... need him to take care of the bankers, the loans, and the debt. I *don't* need *you* to whine about him or how hard things are." Angela's retort was sharp. "These last years have been a disaster. For now, I'm trying not to drown."

Startled, Ellie blinked back tears; a current of something like electricity coursed through her. How could anyone know her fear of a sniper's bullet, a foot across a trip wire, or bad timing of a mortar attack. How could she tell anyone she *needed, wanted* comfort from another *live* human?

Ellie swallowed her hurt, fell silent, and then said, "I know we've all got to pick up our share. It's only that I want him here with me." Her voice trailed off.

"Actually, I don't know what I want," she said. "If I'm truthful with myself, I want everything to be like it was. I want him to love me like he once did."

"He's going to dump on me, on both of us," Angela said. "I feel it. No support. No thank you. Nothing. Seems the Holcombe men are alike, they use whoever or whatever, and move on without even looking back."

Ellie squeezed the phone silently then spoke in a low voice. "Something is way wrong. I feel it."

"Well, honey, honestly, I intend to use whatever guilt he's carrying to get through the next few months. With him working the fields and handling the workers, we might be able to break even. At least this year. Probably nothing extra to apply to the mortgage."

Ellie nodded as if Angela could see her through the phone line. A throbbing began in her temples. She closed her eyes and lightly massaged her temples; grateful Angela could not see her.

Angela continued. "As a kid I was jealous. He was the favored son. Later, I begrudged his taking off for college, marrying you, and then shipping to Vietnam. He used that as an excuse. Dumped *everything* and left. I resented his freedom, his status to do whatever he wanted."

"I don't think he ever meant for you to feel that way," Ellie said, eyes closed, head beginning to throb.

Angela cleared her throat. "When I think back on the times he stood up for me, gave male approval, and I'm ashamed. I'm glad he made it home whole."

A vague sense of disconnect floated through Ellie. "Yes, whole. Came home…whole."

"You know," Angela continued, "Daddy

deliberately set us apart like bugs in a display case and watched."

"Reid and your daddy are alike in opposite ways, the old yin and yang thing. The two of them related by fighting. Besides, your dad was too damaged to be kind, much less loving."

"I know. I think that was the only way he could feel anything. Especially after Mother left."

They sat silent again, each lost in another time and place.

After a long moment, Ellie cleared her throat and spoke. "Reid handles everything like a fight that he has to win. I'm running out of energy. But dern it all, he's *still* my husband and I *still* love him. At least, I do today." She paused, reflected a moment, then went on. "I have responsibility to him. I owe him something. I want to untangle whatever is left between us."

"Know what I remember?" asked Angela. "Daddy had plowed the garden and hitched that molly mule to the tobacco sled for years. He cussed her stubbornness constantly. Reid got fed up and bought a tractor. Once it came, Daddy didn't use that molly again. He lost his feel for the land, that blood-and-flesh connection with the earth. Lost us too."

Ellie opened her eyes, anger rising in a warm flush. She swallowed her impulse to shriek. She leaned forward, arms on the desk, and mentally stared into Angela's face. "Listen to me, Sister-in-law. Here's what I do know: You're strong. You have grit. You're a fine artist. A solid teacher. And you're a resourceful woman. I'm sure Reid loves you, loves the farm, and will eventually help."

Behind her, Marvin Gaye crooned on the radio, his

words looped in the air—mine no longer, not supposed to cry. She flicked the radio off. She and Reid had loved dancing. Now music tugged at her, reminded her of happier times.

"He's changed," Angela said.

"Meaning?"

Angela sighed and took a deep breath. "He seems weather beaten. Damaged. Jumps at me for any and everything. Little stuff."

"Really? Like what?"

"Like clinking dishes. Why, just the other morning, he accidently stepped on that ginger tom's tail. It yowled and Reid hit the floor. *The floor*," she said. "He got up and stomped out the door."

"Can you talk with him?"

"Bless his heart, no. At least not about anything that matters," Angela said. "Mostly he stays aloof, hardly speaks, or gets sullen, clams up. Like he's not here, but some other place."

"Seems life changes things without telling us." Ellie struggled against the rumpled, ugly feeling of the day. "Did he say anything about us? Me and him?"

"Nothing."

She bowed her head, thought of Reid's affinity for the land despite his desperate struggle to leave the farm. "I can tell he's carrying something around. Hurting inside. Work in the field with that tobacco might help. Something physical and solid to focus on."

"He'll probably be by your place sooner or later," Angela said. "We're sharing the truck until he gets settled. He says he'll eventually buy wheels. I feel overwhelmed. Worn out."

"That truck links y'all. Ties you to the land, to Jim

Guy, and your teen years."

"Yeah, it's a good old eggbeater—even with those bald tires." She chuckled.

"Do you think I should drive out to the farm? Talk with him?"

"Not sure. We're still family, not much of one. Barely connected."

"Summer's a busy time for both of us. I'm swamped with tourists, updated brochures, and that Gullah Project. You've got the tobacco and eventually your school contract. Still, I want to see him. *Need* to see him."

"I don't know what to tell you," Angela said.

"I'll wait one or two days to give him time, then try." Ellie sighed. "One thing for certain, there's no shortage of work."

They sat silent, pondering.

Ellie heard Angela take a deep breath and let it out. "Ellie, one other thing."

"What?"

"You've got to make some decision regarding Diana."

"Diana Welsch? What about her?"

Chapter 8
Conversation and Conflict

March 1970

"Yes, Diana Welsch." Angela's voice grew steady. "You and Reid are considered a married couple. People here expect him to act married. Have some feelings about the miscarriage. Pick up on the farm where Daddy quit."

The silence hung between them.

"Talk and speculation will get started soon enough with him staying here instead of with you," Angela said. "Add Diana to the mix and the town gossips will get sore jaws trying to keep up. Nothing takes long in a small town."

Damn small-town gossips anyway."

"Hold on, honey. "You have your job to protect. And, like it or not, the Holcombe name. You owe us that much. Besides, you're a preacher's daughter and folks have certain expectations."

Ellie paused, and twisted the phone cord around her hand, released it, and grew sharp.

"Diana and I work together. On the Chamber's Gullah project. She's a hired consultant. The whole project's for tourism. And historical preservation. That's all."

Ellie reflected on their shared companionship,

cooking together, talking late into the night, and the drama of theater.

"Don't snap at me. There's more than that to this thing. I'm only calling it like it is," Angela said.

"I don't know what you think you know. After all, I'm in Beaufort and you're in Willington."

"Honey don't hand me that crock. I'm not a fool nor am I blind. Her living on that island and you in town hides nothing. The two of you spending every weekend together. You're way too chummy. Only reason you haven't openly moved in together is Reid."

Ellie grew quiet, clenched her teeth.

"Those of us left behind have to handle much more than we ever thought we could or that we're given credit for," Angela said. "Seems like stuff gets dished on your plate and there's nothing to do but take care of it."

"Yeah." Ellie swallowed, unable to keep the knot in her chest from growing tighter. "Thanks, Angela, for calling. You're more than a sister-in-law. But there are some things I have to handle alone."

Angela paused, reflected quietly, and said, "Okay. I guess all said and done, we're going to survive one way or another."

After she hung up, Ellie stared at the stack of papers on her desk, picked up a draft flier, and looked at it blankly. She could see Reid, his crooked smile and muscle-roped arms. She cherished his sense of humor, his penchant for old movies, and enthusiasm for eating popcorn. She opened her desk drawer, rummaged around for aspirin, popped two, and washed them down with coffee. She flipped the radio on again. "Hey Jude" filled the room.

****

A rough vertigo surrounded her and Diana, tangled her feelings, and muddied her thinking.

When Ellie married Reid and graduated from Clemson, she thought she'd never find a job. Then, the wife of a fellow Marine moving to their next duty station, tipped her off to the open Chamber position. With Reid still at Parris Island and scheduled there for specialized training too, Ellie applied immediately.

She liked Beaufort with its old-world city charm and brackish estuaries. Even more than that, she relished working with the Gullah people. The local markets displayed their handmade toys, leather goods, and regional items. The handmade baskets, originally used to winnow rice from chafe, were morphing into works of art, prices increasing monthly.

As a preacher's daughter, she was accustomed to moving frequently, but with her father in an Oregon church, a place she had never lived, she opted to stay in South Carolina. She told herself she'd be fine for the months while Reid was gone, that the time would pass quickly, and he'd return safely.

She launched herself into the Chamber's Gullah-Geechee Cultural Project with abandon. The project stretched along the sea island coast from north Florida to the southern boundary of North Carolina. She consulted with counterpart staff in other states and enjoyed a growing network of colleagues. The potential growth of the sea islands, tenacious survival of coastal families, and lack of basic education for the children offered a mixed bag. If the project brought in tourist dollars, she hoped to leverage attention and funds for the South Carolina schools and infrastructure.

Still, despite thinking herself self-reliant, an overpowering sense of confusion and free-fall descended when Reid shipped. She was alone, really alone for the first time ever.

When she realized she was pregnant, she grew radiant. Even Angela overlooked their earlier differences, gravitated to her, and became warmer.

She lost the baby three months into Reid's deployment and her days dissolved into routines that required no thinking. People either ignored her, deliberately not mentioning Reid nor the lost baby, or they surrounded her with long faces and comments meant to comfort. Instead, everything exacerbated her sense of aloneness.

With Jim Guy's accident and the need to support Angela, the last of Ellie's emotional reserves evaporated and feelings gnawed on her. Reid's infrequent letters stopped. She groped at spider webs. Anger consumed her while she and Diana slipped further into an emotional quagmire.

Chapter 9
Gullah-Geechee Project

February 1965

Decades prior, the Civil War swept south, and sea island owners had deserted their slaves on the rice and indigo plantations. Most slaves stayed on the islands, and in 1861, became some of the first liberated blacks when Northern armies pronounced them "freedmen." No longer considered property, they were rechristened "workers" for the Union, albeit without pay or status.

Fascinated with the African American coastal heritage and Gullah since her senior year at Clemson, Ellie worked on the renovation of the original Beaufort market sheds. The sheds, first built in the 1830s, had received attention by various Chambers since the late '60s. They were becoming a solid tourist attraction.

Lowcountry food traditions and unique cultural-religious customs also revitalized the corridor as Mom and Pop shops opened along the highways. Medium sized restaurants and tourist stopovers sprang up. Ellie worked to keep the growth going.

The Sea Islands corridor, from Florida's St. Johns River to the Carolina Santee River, formed the grant landscape. Beaches stretched down the Atlantic side, shaping an ocean playground. Marshes dominated the channel-pathways facing the mainland.

As a long-limbed youngster, and newcomer to Beaufort, Ellie had wandered across the sawgrass prairies, dug clams, and scavenged for low tide treasures during her first years in junior high. She swatted mosquitos, scratched their bites into sores, and picked grass-cut scabs off her legs while she prowled the mud flats and fishing coves. She learned swamp ways before she explored the school or the town—both as an afterthought.

In high school, she met Reid through their debate teams' competition. She had a fierce penchant for back-and-forth discussions, often leading her group to victory. He'd walk over after the debate, congratulate her, and vow to win the next competition.

Out of curiosity, she made it a point to attend the Beaufort home court basketball games against Willington. Too shy to speak to him before the adrenaline-charged sports crowd, she hung back, and left as soon as the game was over.

When her father accepted a church assignment in Willington, they moved inland. She entered high school and became part of Reid and Angela's world by default.

Ellie quickly learned Reid was constantly surrounded by a covey of girls vying for his attention. Already acquainted from earlier debate team competition, she kept her distance and watched him with interest.

She finished high school in time for her father to take a ministry in Oregon and move west. She enrolled in college and moved north to Boston. After all, she told herself, she was an independent woman.

As an adult, like the Gullah abandoned years before, she found herself at loose ends when Reid shipped. On her own reconnaissance, she mustered inner reserves and built herself a niche. Although she developed friendships with the island people, she was alone, and, to her surprise, lonely.

****

Under a 1968 grant from the historical commission, Diana Welsch, a consultant out of Washington state, hired on as the Chamber's project leader. Quickly submerged in the Gullah's culture, she found their sweetgrass baskets, speech patterns, and crafts exquisite.

When Diana arrived to guide the project, Ellie liked her, finding her capable and perceptive. They immediately collaborated and began a flurry of grant writing. Some days they huddled over reports in the Beaufort offices and worked late, leaving Diana a ten o'clock drive home. Other times, they collected data along the Edisto coast with the late drive home falling on Ellie.

One Wednesday, they finished at midnight, too late for Ellie to drive back to Beaufort. Diana suggested she stay over.

They had shared leftover lasagna and red wine, and talked into the wee morning hours, one propped against a chair, the other leaning on a ragged couch. Two bottles later, they had fallen asleep on the floor intertwined among the cushions.

Sometime during the night, Diana had abandoned the floor and crawled into her bed, leaving Ellie alone. The next morning, at full light, Ellie rose with a crick in her neck, made coffee, and called the office saying, "I plan to spend another day in the field."

Awakened by coffee smells, Diana popped into the

kitchen, hugged Ellie good morning, and vanished into a hot shower.

Several nights and three bottles of red wine later, they consummated their budding relationship, flowing seamlessly into its labyrinth, not fully acknowledging the social taboos nor clandestine lifestyles. They grew closer, shared books, leftover dinners, and time.

Ellie introduced Diana to the tidal marshes, cane-pole fishing, and the sun-tangy flavors of Spanish-Caribbean Lowcountry cooking.

Diana loved much of the coastal life. She often rode her bike on rambling explorations along the coastline. Sometimes Ellie accompanied Diana, sometimes not.

The two-house arrangement and a few separate interests worked well, allowing time together and time apart, thus accommodating both work and socializing.

After a few months, the Beaufort rental became a shared work-living space whenever Diana had to stay in town. Ellie decide to spruce the house up. An odd collection of friends painted the inside. A few hired craftspeople replaced rotted porch wood, and repaired window screens. They called their collective work, remodeling parties. Ellie signed a rent-to-purchase agreement.

With one bedroom, galley-sized kitchen, dining alcove, and single bath, the tiny place took on a raw energy. Friends spread sleeping bags on any available floor space staying over Friday and Saturday nights sharing potlucks and talking politics and street demonstrations late into the evening.

"Might as well be comfortable and enjoy the place," she said when Angela commented on putting money into a rental not yet hers. Ellie teased Angela into a better mood, proclaiming her "resident artist" and asking her to choose colors for the outside trim and inside details.

Pleased, Angela finally acquiesced and suggested haint blue to keep spirits away. After all, she opined, "Ghosts are plentiful among the islands and in the marshes. Small haint children are only mischievous while haint men can prove treacherous." To emphasize her point, Angela insisted in a husky voice that a bottle tree—a dead tree with blue bottles stuck on sawed off branches—be placed in the front yard to ward off additional evil.

In folklore tradition, she explained, "The blue of water and sky creates a crossing between earth and heaven, between the living and dead. Haints and spirits, roaming around, see the blue bottles, think they are pretty, and climb inside. They get stuck, can't get out, and evaporate in the hot sun."

Occasionally Angela dropped by on weekday afternoons. She'd work and leave soon after supper saying, "Willington's almost an hour's drive and farm chores keep hollering." She never came on Sundays.

Gradually, with the repairs complete, Ellie and Diana had explored life along the Sea Islands. They thought of themselves as soul mates and never meant to fall into a deeper relationship. It simply happened.

Chapter 10
Random Thoughts, Slow Dissolve

March 1970

Without letters, Reid effectively disappeared from Ellie's life until three years later, his tours completed, the Marines shipped him back to South Carolina. By that time, so much had changed she couldn't keep details sorted. His face, his smell, his rakishness had begun a slow dissolve. She could no longer hear his voice or feel his essence. Guilt piled up. With Diane in the mix, Ellie was powerless to recapture him.

She stumbled through the days acutely aware of her anxiety, a missing piece, a repeating transitory feeling. She worked overtime, thankful that the Chamber's Gullah grant was complex and consuming and required researching early-to-late.

Tourists filing through the Chamber offices interrupted her grant work but also provided comic relief. An Iowa farm family of four dropped by the agency several days running, questions spilling out as soon as they entered the door.

What are the best restaurants serving Lowcountry food? Where to buy handwoven baskets? How do you get to the marshland locations to see birds? The father wanted nothing except to fish, saying, "I dern well didn't need to sightsee."

The pre-teen boys groused about "Where can we find pirate doubloons? What about Confederate war treasure?"

Ellie laughed at their squabbling; they were so unabashedly awestruck by the town and sea. Besides, they offered a respite from the writing and her no-mail worries around Reid.

At night Ellie collapsed into the comfort of Rosie and Grover. And wine.

Then Angela confessed. "I can't see Jim Guy's face anymore. It's fading. I can't even recall his smile. I can barely see him walking around the farm with that lopsided gait of his."

She threw herself into sketching his hands and face, a desperate attempt to hold him. Reams of sketch studies stacked up on her kitchen table.

Ellie relied on photos, all taken before Reid had shipped. She scrambled to rebuild her memories of him, to recapture the details of his face, his voice, but most of all, their joy.

Now with Reid flying in from Nam, Ellie moved through the days as if underwater.

Chapter 11
Thanksgiving

November 1969

Ellis's sleepless nights and fears for Reid's safety depleted her energy and creativeness. By November with the two funerals during the previous months and her lack of letters, she vowed she'd break the crying cycle.

She invited Angela to Beaufort for Thanksgiving dinner saying, "Reading seed catalogues only offers so much defense against the doldrums. It's Thanksgiving. Bring any stray that's got no other place to go. Children okay too. We're having Cajun turkey."

A fellow teacher along with Jon, her ten-year old son, came with Angela. The trio drove down U.S. 15 rather than the Interstate, slowing in the small towns to comment on the mom-and-pop stores and antique shops before they picked up speed outside the communities, again passing farmland, tobacco curing barns, and grazing cows. With two-lane curving roads, the drive took longer but road bingo kept Jon entertained. Eventually, he tired of the game and suggested they sing along to the radio. They cranked the volume up and belted out the latest-protest songs, albeit off-key.

For her part, Ellie invited a couple from down the street, their four children, and Diana Welsch.

Tall and angular, Diana moved with the liquid grace of an athlete. An avid cyclist back from a two-week road trip, she exuded health and energy, drawing Ellie to her with physicality and independence.

Diana arrived late Tuesday afternoon before Thanksgiving and immediately threw herself into decorating the house with real pumpkins, fall leaves, orange candles, and a horn of plenty centerpiece for the main table. She dropped by Big Discount Carolina for Thanksgiving napkins, small plates, and plastic glasses. On a whim, she bought a cutout tom turkey with paper tail fanned wide for the children's table.

Ellie had started thawing their feast and doing prep work early Wednesday. She measured Cajun spices for a rub, planned dirty rice, chopped fresh cranberry relish, and set out fixings for a green bean casserole.

Mid-afternoon Thursday, Angela and her fellow teacher with Jon arrived grinning from ear to ear after their driving adventure. Known in the local community for her butter flake crusts, Angela brought her homemade pies, two each of pecan and sweet potato. Other guests dribbled in bringing various vegetable dishes and finger nibbles.

With the day sunny-crisp, the gaggle of kids and guests trooped out to the back yard. Adults carried drinks and snacks and spread the treats out along the picnic table.

Jon, carrying potato chips and dip, spotted a heart carved in the table. He traced the awkward image with his finger, reading aloud, "Look what someone left. 'April 1965. Reid + Ellie.' Who are they?"

The group, munching tidbits chuckled at the question. Angela, roaring with laughter, sprayed chewed chips across the table.

Ellie's neighbor shifted to smile at her before teasing, "Only high school sweethearts leave initials in public. Want to tell us more?"

Feeling her face grow warm, Ellie stalled, handed out paper plates, and kept repeating, "It's nothing. Nothing. Besides, it's not public. It's my backyard."

Had it been four years ago she and Reid, lust so strong, she could still taste the saltiness? Could feel passion swell-up in her loins, the terrible pressure of it, and finally, a wet relief shuddering through her?

"It's a puzzle yet to be solved. Like Fred," Angela said.

"Fred who?"

"A-fred of the big bad wolf." Everyone groaned.

Ellie mouthed a 'thank you' to Angela.

"That's corny," Jon said. He grabbed a hand full of chips and drifted away to join the other children.

Diana cocked her head and reached for a glass of iced tea. "We don't drink tea sweetened in the North like you do here. Think that's why you talk so slow and syrupy?"

The husband of Ellie's neighbor, raised his glass and said, "Bless your little Yankee heart, I think you're on to something." Everyone laughed good-naturedly and saluted with their raised glasses.

The children scattered across the yard with a game of dodge ball while the adults talked school issues, embroidered on local gossip, speculated about politics, and laughed at knock-knock jokes.

By four with dusk settling, Ellie suggested the gathering move inside and spread out along the cherry wood dining table. Kids, delighted with their own space, clustered around a folding card table set up in the kitchen with the turkey cutout.

Despite her slightly over-spiced turkey and too crusty sage dressing, Ellie tickled the gathering by serving champagne and offering a celebratory first toast. The cheerful noise continued as the crowd heaped their plates and bestowed accolades for the potluck dishes.

After dinner, to Ellie's surprise, Angela and Diana spent time together in the front porch swing talking and sipping bubbly. Not until the call for pie and coffee did they come in, giddy and laughing, still exchanging North vs South tales.

After dessert, kids watched television while the adults cleared the kitchen and divided leftovers for their take-home boxes. Twice Angela got a bit teary-eyed about Jim Guy but rallied and the party did not falter.

No one mentioned Reid. Like scraps of paper, their plans had disappeared, fluttered for a heartbeat on a snag, before blowing away, leaving them vaguely stunned as if by a too loud clap of thunder.

Sometimes, she wished him dead in Vietnam—only to wither from guilt at the thought.

Chapter 12
Terrell Family Farm

May 1970

In ragged parts and pieces over the next week, Reid realized Angela was right. Raising tobacco was multilayered, the times changing, and agriculture markets shifting. They had to break even this season to salvage anything. He stopped by Mary and Calvin's farm mid-afternoon.

Their place, five acres including the clapboard house, nestled in a cluster of trees, mostly oaks with several pecan trees and a black walnut on the east side. A farrowing pen and shoat enclosure sat behind the house with a vegetable garden taking a chunk of the remaining land.

As was customary among country folk, Reid sat in the pickup and popped the horn. At the sound, Mary pushed open the screen door and stepped on the porch, still drying her hands on the cotton apron.

Her cinnamon face broke into a smile when she recognized him. "Lordy goodness, is that you Reid? She finished wiping her hands and placed them on her hips.

Reid stepped out of the truck.

"I praised the Lord when my Joe made it in. Then I hear you coming home too, and I sing Lord's praises again." She spoke in the rapid patois of her Gullah heritage.

Reid's face blushed warm at Mary's sincerity.

She continued, smiling as she spoke. "Angela and Ellie are torn up with all the things happening they see on the news. They upset over the homecoming you folks had to deal with what with marches and all. You back safe and that there's good news all around."

"Thanks. Nice to be here." He fumbled a moment with his John Deere cap, and then asked, "Calvin and Joe around?"

"They both down there with them hawgs." She waved her hand to a path twisting between several outbuildings. "They foolin with that sow. Feeding, I think."

"You don't mind, I'll walk out and see them."

"Don't mind. You gwine on down. Joe be glad see you here. Calvin too. You ain't no stranger, you hear? No stranger." She wiped her hands again, smiled, and stepped back inside.

He started to the barns as a flirting breeze rose, the scent of honeysuckle light among the weeds and tall grasses. Tree leaves shaded the path as if shining through burlap.

Working their small farms and growing plants of their choice gave the Terrell family independence. They didn't grow sugar cane, cotton, or tobacco—considering them plantation owner cash crops. They planted only what they could eat, a legacy from slave allotment gardens.

Tomatoes, turning red, and pole beans covered the bamboo stakes. Yellow okra blossoms sprinkled color in the network of cucumbers and squash. Before fall, the garden would be stripped and replanted with turnips and sweet potatoes.

The hogs, considered figurative piggy banks, added to the Terrell income. Mary's job at Noe's Bakery and Calvin's day labor brought in cash to purchase gas, flour, sugar, and utilities, things they could not raise themselves. Hog money gave them extras.

Reid saw Joe leaning against the top rail of a pig pen feeding the market shoats. Pretty Sal, their bluetick hound, rose and bawled, announcing his approach.

Joe, glancing up at the commotion, recognized Reid, and sat the empty bucket next to a post. A vague sense of disquiet settled on him whenever whites were around. He resented being treated as if uneducated, a non-person. He watched Reid approach, and, finally, as an afterthought, spoke.

"What brings you out here to the black side of the county?"

"Checking up on you." Reid pulled a toothpick out of his shirt pocket and stuck it in his mouth.

"Checking on me? You mean checking for them chickens that disappeared outta your coop? Hell, man, you too late. I done fried them up. They real tasty." Joe faced his neighbor, arms crossed on his chest, and pushed against the imprecise boundaries between them. Since Reid had stopped by and was on Terrell property, Joe knew Reid wanted something.

Reid backed up a step at Joe's greeting, narrowed his eyes, and stared.

Breaking the tension with a half-smile, Joe gestured Reid forward. "Ah, come on man. I'm funning with you."

Reid glared, half paused, and then continued to

walk toward Joe.

"Don't think you seen Pappy since we got back," Joe said.

"Nope. Sure haven't." Still prickly from the ribbing, Reid spoke in a flat tone.

"Come on. Say hello. Take a look at Pappy's sow. She's pure Duroc. Due to farrow sometime next week."

They fell into step toward a shaded area under a tree. A stooped man in overalls leaned on the pen railing. Pretty Sal plunked down by him, her tail thumping in the dust.

Reid looked at the man's nappy gray thatch and reflected on the toll war levied. Seemed no one escaped.

Calvin grinned, moved forward several steps, and wiped his hands on a red bandana.

"My good gawd. Look here now. It's Reid Holcombe. Glad you home. Yes, sir, glad both y'all made it home safe." He continued wiping his hands and gestured at a pig rooting in a trough. "Look at my sow. This here her third litter. Usually has ten or more. She a good one for taking care them piglets."

"Nice long back," Reid said. "Didn't realize you had a purebred. What do you do with the gilts?"

"Well, I mostly sells or trades them to my neighbors. Once't in a while, I keep one, but I only got so much room and can't take on too many hawgs. Besides, Mary after me to retire. How a black man gonna retire from farming?"

"How does anyone retire? Farming's a hard life," Reid said.

"Well I reckon that 'bout right. Get that dirt in you veins, you always be a farmer." Calvin stuffed the red bandana in his bib overalls pocket. "Not much for folks like me but sharecropping."

"Sharecropping's not farming," Joe said. "It's a made-up white word for 'you do the sweat, I get the money.'"

Reid stiffened.

Calvin inched forward. "Y'alls both over in Nam same time. Yes, sirrah, all working together in that jungle. We work together here too. Especially since we all work in the dirt."

"Not me. I ain't be no farmer," Joe said, "and I sure not gonna be no Marine lifer."

"What the hell were you doing over there?" Reid asked.

"Humph." Joe snorted and crossed his arms. "After cops shot up the brothers at Orangeburg—and that was a *state* university—I needed to do something. I was damn lucky. Especially since I happened to be up visiting that weekend and almost got caught up in that fracas."

"For chrissake." Reid's face glowed hot, eyes narrowed, and fists clenched at his side. "From what I heard, they were rioting."

"We got some serious miscommunication going on here." Joe shifted and stood square before Reid.

"Cops shooting up unarmed students—no lie, they killed at least two, wounded over twenty—and you think *they* were rioting?" Joe shook his head and spoke in a hard voice. "I decided Vietnam would be safer than college. At least I'd have a gun. Why'd you go?"

Reid rigid, his jaw muscle bugling, snorted. "Volunteered." He took a deep breath, relaxed slightly, and said, "Supposed to be my way out, off the farm, out of town."

Nervous, Calvin shifted from one foot to another, cleared his throat, and said, "You hear my boy here going to Boston come September as an activist? He gonna help with that desegregation mess and civil rights stuff before he starts to Howard University up to the capitol. You know, Washington. He keep working for what's right, too." Calvin's voice rose with pride.

"That so?" Reid studied Joe. Muscular and coffee-colored, Joe lounged against a post, broad arms resting on the board fence, hands dangling open.

"Boston? Activist? Could be rough up there," Reid said.

"No rougher than here. Could be things are changing. I'm gonna be part of it." Joe's voice still had an edge.

"Why go up there?"

"Gotta get outta here. South draws the meanest line between people. I have a better chance up North," Joe said.

"Better chance for what?"

"Making a difference. Getting an education. *Surviving*." Joe continued to lean against the fence.

"Yankees kill you as dead as southerners." Reid slid his hands into his pockets, his lanky form knotted with tension.

"That's what I'd expect you to say." Joe straightened, stood taller. "You no better than any other honkey strutting around talking how we all 'look alike.' Spouting about knowing 'my place.' That's nothing but common racist trash talk." Joe's face twisted with resentment, sweat glistened on his forehead.

The two men glared at each other, black and white

mirror images bound by social circumstance and home.

Hands outstretched in front of him, palms open, Calvin motioned downward. His face took on a new series of worry-lines as he stepped forward, still motioning down.

"Y'all wait a minute. Let's us not get all roostered up and feathers flared. You boys done gone through same mud and killing. Ain't right to be at each other now you home. 'Specially since you both hailing from the same hometown. Things gotta change." He rubbed his dark hands together, pink palms flashing.

Joe deferred to his father and stood silent against the fence. After all, no sense letting whitey see anything but a solid front between him and his parents. He had handled himself that way in Nam, careful to present a united Negro line, which had led to more than one black-white scuffle.

"What brings you out here today?" Calvin asked. "Me and Angela already been working you pappy's farm together. Mary hep out ever chance she get when she not at that bakery job."

Reid took a deep breath and spoke blunt. "Angela says she still needs help, can't keep the place going without Jim Guy. I thought Joe might be interested. Guess not. What with Boston and a university planned."

"You got that right," Joe said, face scrunched.

"Well, I told Angela that." Reid spat the toothpick out. "I told her that very thing. But she still wants to make some kind of arrangement."

"Like what?" Calvin asked.

Joe casually pulled out a pocketknife and whittled at a stick. He kept his eyes on the stick, careful not to look up.

"Regular work." Reid glowered, glanced at Joe, and continued. "Regular, year-round work."

"What 'bout you?" Joe feigned disinterest. "Where you play into on this stuff? I ain't no field hand. Pappy same as me. Got no use for shares."

His gaze fixed on the dark face, Reid slung his words out slow and deliberate.

"I don't want a *sharecropper*. Angela needs someone that can farm. And that she can trust." He crossed his arms again and stood feet planted apart, knees slightly flexed.

"You mean keep under y'alls thumb." Joe closed the pocketknife and slid it back into his pocket, his lips set in a hard line. He flicked the stick away and stared directly into Reid's face.

"No, I don't," Reid said, his voice hard. "Old Man wanted to keep everyone down. Angela's different. Jim Guy too. Angela swears changes are happening. She says agribusiness firms been moving in. Government price supports winding down." Reid stared at his scarred hands, fingers yellowed from smoking.

Joe nodded.

Reid continued in a husky voice. "We've talked about it. I was against doing anything with *you* people. Angela's pushing me. With all the changes going on, I guess I've got to give it a try. Besides, I owe her."

"I done explained I got other plans. Don't need your 'give it a try.'" Joe said.

"Wait a minute. Let's hold on." Again, Calvin spread his hands waist level, patted the air. "Son let the man finish talking. Right now, we listen. Nothing else."

Joe frowned, lines around his eyes crinkled. He stood silent.

Reid ignored Joe and spoke directly to the older man. "You've worked with Angela and Jim Guy when he was alive, so you know what to expect. She needs you regular. Needs you to arrange the summer field crew, keep handling the tobacco, work the corn, and care for what's left of the livestock."

"What's the catch?" Joe asked.

"Year-round work. Not seasonal. No day stuff. Year-round paycheck."

"And that means what?"

"For one thing, it means we can count on each other. Nobody hustles around trying to line up workers competing with everyone else. You get regular pay *all* the time, you get money even in winter. Tobacco starts and you act as straw boss. Keep everyone lined up."

Joe leaned back against the farrowing pen and propped his heel against a post.

The sow snuffed and rooted along the edges of the enclosure. A breeze ruffled the tree leaves tweaking the patterns of light and shade. Mid-May humidity weighed heavy and the incessant buzzing of gnats increased.

Reid continued. "Angela wants to stay on the home place. No halves. We handle expenses. You're farmers like your people before you. You Terrell's have always worked the land. You've got this place and Mary's got her job in town. You want, we hire Joe as day labor this summer until he leaves in September."

"Sounds like fancy sharecropper-double-talk to me." Joe grunted, shifted his gimp leg, and stood; arms crossed.

"You rockhead. We're offering straight-up salary, income all year."

"You still ain't said where you figure in."

The three men stood silent. A passing breeze barely stirred the air. Pretty Sal lumbered away from the trio and flopped down in deeper shade. Several yard chickens scratched about for dropped grain before wandering toward the garden. The shoats rooted in the dampness.

Reid removed his cap, ran a hand through his hair, and replaced the cap. He shook his head before he spoke.

"I don't want that farm. Soon's the tobacco's sold and as much debt as possible paid down, I'm moving on. Angela wants to stay. She sees this as her home."

"What Pappy and me to do about those spit-and-scratch crackers hanging out? Specially them running around in bedsheets. They likely to kill the likes of us 'cause they can," Joe said. "Especially when they think we're keeping a white man from getting anything, even if it's worthless."

"I know," Reid said. "The big growers have already contacted us. Said they'd give us preferential treatment *if we sell.*"

"Sorta like the white boys in Nam got preferential duty and all us got the honeypot burning details twice as often. One of those get out of jail free cards, that it?" Joe leaned forward and spat.

The elderly man watched Reid's face grow tense, saw his pupils dilate, and heard his ragged breath. Calvin touched Joe's arm and inclined his head no.

Reid ran a hand across his shirt, realized he was breathing in gulps. He swallowed, his nostrils flared at the faint stench of raw sewage and latrine burning duty. Diesel fuel, the key ingredient for burning honeypot waste, sent choking plumes of smoke into the sky.

Whites took latrine duty usually as punishment for some infraction, while it was a routine assignment for blacks. Reid clenched his fists.

Slowly, he looked back at Calvin and quivered from the adrenaline jack-up. He swallowed and concentrated on fence splinters, whine of insects, hog perfume, and the sun cooking down. He swallowed again.

"You right 'bout Jim Guy and Angela," Calvin said quietly. "Them two acts like my Mary, taking care of everybody else first. 'Specially Jim Guy. He was a good man." He tapped Joe's arm lightly, then snugged his hands between his bib and shirt, hooked his thumbs in the straps, and continued. "I needs talk it over with my Mary. Joe got his own plans. He make his own decision. I think on this offer a spell."

Reid shook his head, took a deep breath, and refocused. "That's right. Y'all think about it. Angela wants to stay. I want to leave."

"You gotta be braced for serious fallout when you talk regular work with likes of us," Joe said.

"My boy's right. We'd be fools not to be set for meanness," Calvin said.

"*All* of us better be braced."

The men watched the sow root in the mud and then lay lengthwise in the coolness, her big belly extended. Flies buzzed over the wallow, moved in zigzagging flights.

"Think about it." Reid glanced again at the sow, nodded to Calvin, and eyeballed Joe hard. "I'll see you next week after that sow farrows."

No one extended a hand.

Reid crunched down the path to the pickup. Pretty

Sal trotted alongside, stopping to sniff in the weeds as part of her escort duty.

He climbed into the truck, opened the glove box, and fingered an onionskin envelope. Before he shipped, he recognized signs that he and Ellie were potentially in danger of unraveling. After she miscarried, she wrote with less feeling, less often. She sent a photograph of herself, standing alone on the beach, unsmiling. The letters were a lifeline home—to which he could not respond. Gradually her letters dwindled.

Chapter 13
Eleanor Holcombe

April 1967

Ellie could not sleep the first nights after Reid shipped. Sometimes she'd drift off only to startle awake in a cold sweat, her body aching from tension.

Those fragmented nights, she stared down at herself from some place overhead, her mind meandering. Her loyalties, mistakes, and desires unspooled in a hard knot of confusion. How to balance the days in Boston, her nights with Reid, and now, this passion for Diana? Her joy and disappointments worried her as much with things that happened, as things that did not happen.

Around five, she got up, splashed water on her face, and made coffee. As soon as it perked, she sat in the swing and nursed a cup until the sun rose. Grover, always the wise soul, lay on the plank floor, head on his paws, and eyes fixed on her face. Occasionally he'd thump his tail on the porch, as if punctuating a thought.

She had burned deep inside, feeling hollow and alone. Growing up in the South, she'd learned not to be too honest, to swallow her opinions and not choke, and mingle at social gatherings without discussing race or politics. She learned not to take sides in public, to appear uninterested in anything except fashion and how to cook a pot roast. When she had moved north, she discovered complex layers labeled *me* and found a new self.

At daybreak, Grover got up, stretched, yawned, and snuffed around the perimeter of the house. His patrol concluded, he sat on the sidewalk waiting for the paperboy to toss the *Carolina News.*

Ellie took the paper inside, fed the cat, set kibbles out for Grover, and dressed for work. An assistant director at the Chamber, she put on her neutral face, donned a navy skirt-suit with low heels, and assumed a business appearance. Today, she added an off-white blouse with tucks, a nod to southern femininity. When talking with her boss or co-workers, she'd laugh, amazed at how quickly she slipped back into deferential and gracious after Wellesley.

Months earlier at her father-in-law's grave, she had watched a Carolina wren hopping from bush to bush, its twilled notes more comforting than the Baptist minister's eulogy. Angela had chosen a brief graveside service in deference to the Old Man's hostility toward religion and his alienation of neighbors over the last years. Despite the early spring crispness, the modest carnations wilted along the casket edges. A cluster of people stood to the side with solemn expressions, occasionally whispering among themselves. Each would shake hands or hug and murmur "I'm so sorry" as they filed past the grave, a ritual meant to comfort the bereaved.

After the service, Ellie left the gaping hole and drove toward the Santee River watershed. At the bay turn out, she parked, pulled her heels and panty hose off, tossed them into the car, and then ambled to a cove suspended between sea and sky. She sank down on the cool sand and listened to the water's relentless movement.

She sobbed and screamed Reid's name, repeatedly threw it skyward until she grew hoarse. Later she stood, arms outstretched, red curls tangling in the wind, and whispered, "Come home, my love, *come home.*"

The ocean, a microscopic birthing place and sometimes grave, heaved in tidal lock steps. Shore birds sprinted past, busy with their avian workday, and left white squirts on the sand.

The incoming tide erased her footprints, rolled seaward, pulled parts of her beyond the Carolina barrier islands and on toward Vietnam. She had stared down at the watery touch. Did Reid, a world away, feel the same wetness pulling him and dissolving his love?

Chapter 14
Eau de Opossum

March 1970

Ellie sniffed the air as if something rotten surrounded her, strong, like a dead opossum. A whiff that sort of floats out before the stink hits, and the sound of flies buzzing over a greasy patch of ground, registers. Eventually the carcass dissolves, musk dissipates, and grass grows again. But it takes a long time.

Her morning, still fragile, started pleasantly enough with fresh coffee on the patio with Grover and Rosie. While they ate kibbles, she drank a second cup, then dressed, and drove to work.

The minute she opened the office door, saw the brochure proofs spread all over her desk, a hint of dead-opossum-day floated toward her. Custodians had knocked the folder off the desk into the mop bucket. They'd picked everything up, laid it out in sheets across the desk and chair. Pages were smeared and unreadable.

Everything dried overnight but most pages were crinkled, stuck together, or out of order. The janitors left a note offering apologies and saying they would come by later. The lost time and effort sucked the breath out of her, made her frantic with the printer's Friday deadline looming. Another trace of dead possum day.

As she finished putting a few pages in order, the phone rang. One of the clerks called in sick. She started gathering the brochure again and the boss phoned, explaining he had a meeting he'd forgotten to mention, and would not be in until after two. She went back to sorting.

Ellie managed to finish the cover section when the door buzzer sounded. A family of six came in, requested maps and brochures, historical sites, and the best places to eat. On a budget. No high-dollar tourist stuff. Requests, slung at her in rapid-fire order, hung in the air as the family stressed only one day for everything.

Cramming. Looming deadlines. Her and Reid. Opossum stink. The door buzzer went off again as a young couple walked in appearing lost.

****

Almost two o'clock before the boss got in from his meeting and Ellie could spring loose for lunch. She didn't feel hungry but desperately needed a break and the spring weather called her. Anxious about attempting to salvage the brochure edits, mulling over what to do about Reid, how to support Angela, and balancing her work on the Gullah Project pulled at her. And, of course, decisions about Diana. Always Diana. And now, Reid.

Ellie hurried down the street to SandWitches and Subs, ordered a burger-bacon melt, and made a mental note to phone Off-Set Printing for the latest mark-ups. She needed to chat with Angela about Reid, the tobacco work, and the farm mortgage.

Sack in hand, Ellie strolled along Bay Street to

Waterfront Park, her favorite picnic place. Waterfront meandered beside the river, a simple strip park for walking and biking. The combination of the tea-colored river, the piccolo bird chorus, and the endless drama of people passing relaxed her. Even the high-pitched squeals of children playing, usually too piercing, were pleasant.

With lunch spread out on the table, she raised her face to the sun, took a deep breath, and allowed herself to drift.

Twice while Reid was gone, she made origami peace cranes and placed them in the river, releasing them seaward toward Vietnam. Now, with him home, came a worrisome buzz, a fly she could neither catch nor chase away.

She bit into her sandwich, savored the bacon, and noticed Reid rattle by in Jim Guy's pickup. He parked near the Chamber office and walked across the street.

Another sniff of her figurative decaying opossum floated near as she watched him while the morning stress threatened to gag her. She swallowed and laid the sandwich aside uncertain what to expect. Other than the phone call, she hadn't seen nor spoken to him since his return.

Not until Reid stepped onto the grass, did she take a deep breath, and move to him, drawn by his self-assured, stalking-cat stride. He still had a physicality at once gentle and dangerous. Her heart pounded and her mouth seemed filled with cotton. When a few feet separated them, she reached out, stepped into him, and buried her face in his neck inhaling his man sweat.

Reid stood rigid, his arms dangling. Even with her breath on his neck, he made no move to embrace her despite their dizzying, convoluted bond.

"It's good to see you," Ellie said, "to know you're alive and whole. I've worried about you. Missed you." She stared at him and realized the man she was looking at was older than his twenty-seven years.

"What did you think I'd be?" No longer the devil's own jester, he stood stone hard, his voice curt. He did not smile.

She stuttered. "I don't know what to think. You staying with Angela. Not coming home. The lack of letters or calls. Even the postman asked me what had happened to you." She moved back a step, her eyes scanning his face. "I was afraid you'd been killed. One of those missing in action things. Or you were maimed up too bad to get in touch."

"Well, I'm neither." He edged sideways, away from her, shoved his hands in his jeans. "Angela's my damn sister. I grew up in that room. That's my homeplace. I have a right to stay there. Besides, I called you."

"You were halfway back when you called and said, 'don't show up.'" Ellie moved closer and shook her head. "I'm your wife. You're home three days and now you show up? Barely touch me. What does that mean? Talk to me."

"You quit writing." He threw the accusation at her, and stepped toward the river, thumbs in his belt loops. He stood quiet while the tea-dark water flowed seaward. A sense of loss gnawed on his soul, ripped at his memories. He pushed back against memories of early manhood, his beginning with Ellie, and, most of all, the killing and waste in Nam.

"No. That's not true. I wrote," Ellie said. A drained

note crept into her voice. "I wrote the entire time you were over. I wrote until I thought there was no one out there, only my imagination. I began to wonder if you ever really existed." She shook her head. "Reid, I'm your wife. I love you. We have things to resolve." She reached for his hand, sensed her chest contract.

He held her hand, the softness of it, and pulled her into him.

She melted into his body, trembled against his hardness.

His voice splintered. "*Things* happened over there. I *killed*. Took everything they had. They're dead. I'm alive." He brushed her hand away. "I *still see* them."

"Who? What *things*? Tell me. I'm here. I'll listen."

"I can't explain," he said. "Too much. I can't remember. Won't remember."

"Reid, I don't understand. You stay at a farm you don't want. You wait days before you try to see me. And then you show up in a public park and can't even hug me. What is this?"

He stepped away, barked at her. "I have stuff to do."

"Angela says you're like a shadow. I need to know you care. Know our love is still alive."

"Do you love me?" He whirled on her, his lips peeled back from his teeth, eyes black with emotion.

"Yes," she answered in a whisper. "Yes, I love you." She lowered her hands and waited.

A jogger trotted pass. Children played on the grass, their laughter bubbling into the air. Two teenaged girls ambled along on the sidewalk eating chocolate ice cream. An older couple strode hand-in-hand, heads bent toward each other, talking.

"At least now I know you're alive," Ellie said.

"After you lost that baby, I figured you'd go your own way. You didn't need me anymore." His voice softened.

"*You* are my way." Ellie began to cry. At first, only silent tears, then quivering-lips and hands-over-her-face sobs. Her whole body trembled until dry heaves shook her and she gasped for breath.

He watched her, arms limp at his side, from some distant place beyond the park. Images moved around him with the sound of crumbling paper. He shuddered.

The town rattled along with its workday business: Cars ground gears and bumped down brick roads. A pickup belched smoke leaving a trail of gray. Snippets of conversation and disconnected words floated past.

Reid's shoulders slumped. He leaned back slightly and stared at the sky. Finally, he gathered her in his arms, pulled her close, and spoke into her hair.

"Too much has happened too fast. I'm lost. I'm so confused. Feelings are all mixed up."

"Come home. We must settle what's between us. We need each other."

They stood foreheads touching, a thin warmth hovered between them. He caressed her cheek with a calloused hand and traced along her nose with his finger. Her hand fluttered against his chest. They lingered together a moment before he gently pushed her away.

"Too much has happened."

She covered her face and cried again, struggled for self-control, made choking sounds, and nervously wiped at mascara smears on her hand.

"Come home. We need to talk. And *listen* to each

other. Please."

Reid rubbed his hands up and down her arms, and muttered, "Things happened. I'm not the same person. I'm somebody you don't even *want* to know."

She hiccupped and spoke in a frail voice. "I can leave work right now. Meet you at home. We can talk. Too much is *still* happening."

Bicycles whirred along the sidewalk. In the distance, the staccato shouts of boys playing round ball. A dog sniffed at a tree, lifted a leg, squirted, and continued his ramble. The park, a refuge in the clutter of living, pulsated with life.

Reid petted her face, held her gently, and said, "Not today. Maybe later." He kissed her on the forehead.

She flinched. "*Later*? Later? What's *that* supposed to mean?"

He walked away.

Chapter 15
Alone

March 1970

Ellie sat at a picnic table and cried until a woman stopped, offered her a Kleenex, and asked if she should call someone. Flustered, Ellie said no, took the tissue, and wiped at the mascara on her fingers.

She grabbed the uneaten sandwich, wadded it into a ball of bread and mayonnaise, and slammed it into a trashcan on her way out of the park.

Unable to see clearly, she tripped in the grass, her face growing hot at her awkwardness. She continued toward the office.

Exhausted after Reid, she vaguely muttered to the boss she needed to leave. He gave her a quizzical, mute look, and nodded.

Ellie drove straight home. Once there, she flung her pumps across the living room, stomped into the bedroom, yanked clothes off, and left them puddled on the floor. Sitting on the edge of the bed, she cried until there were no more tears. She curled into a ball and lay on the bed 'til evening shadows crept up the walls.

Where was the man that spun her around the dance floor, made her toss her head back laughing? The man who debated for non-violent resistance then *volunteered* for Vietnam?

Finally, with the dark settling, she rose, stumbled into the bathroom, ran water into the claw-foot tub, and sank into the warmth. She sloshed it on her face and lathered up with rose soap, scrubbing at the pain. She lay until the water cooled, got out, slipped into an oversized tee, and padded barefooted into the kitchen, her eyes swollen and sore as if twined in briar vines.

A whiskey over ice with orange peel, a second drink, and a wild montage of emotions bound her in a long rope of lust, bewilderment, and tenderness. She took a deep swallow of a third whiskey, savored its bite, and grew heavy as the alcohol and warm bath relaxed her.

Married before boot camp, she'd stood by Reid through advanced training, did nest building in their rental house, frolicked with him until he shipped, and then written and sent pictures almost daily—at least the first year. Today, he had dismissed her like an errant child, and left the park saying he couldn't talk. His own wife. Three years gone, a few days back home, and he can't talk? Damn his soul.

Staring down at herself from a height, she tried to shake off a sharp stab of anger, and find contentment within an indistinct, lost love. Decisions lined up, each more demanding than the next, creating ambivalence. What to feel? How to manage her inner self? And, what to do with the gnarly question of Diana? Was there even a place for Reid anymore?

At midnight, she crept into bed still wearing the tee. Rosie followed, curled up next to her head, and purred.

Mouth open, Ellie snored despite the stink of dead opossum.

In the morning, she realized she had forgotten to feed Grover.

Chapter 16
Angela Holcombe McAlister

May 1967

Reid had shipped the previous year. Angela and Jim Guy worked the farm, managed the old man's growing anger, and struggled with the financial burdens of an outdated homeplace.

Eight months into 1967, while plowing, the tractor had rolled on Jim Guy. That afternoon when it crushed life from his bulk, Angela harnessed the molly, and hitched her to the tractor. The mule strained and dug in, pulled as if she understood something was bad wrong. By the time Angela got the Ford righted, Jim Guy was dead.

Angela sat. She stared at his body, his great girth, and willed him to get up and lumber toward her. She said his name over and over, an incantation to call back his life. Alone, she cried, stroked his face, and held his great paw of a hand

Birds chirruped in the brambles. The smell of plowed earth settled in her nostrils. The air had a denim color. Not until the mule grunted and rattled her harness, did Angela realize dusk had settled and sweat, dried white, crusted the animal's shoulders.

She laid Jim Guy's hand on his chest, smoothed his shirt collar, and straightened his legs. Stiff from sitting, she stood and spoke aloud. "I need to tell Ellie. She'll know what to do. I have to call the sheriff too." Muttering to herself, she had stumbled away, leading the mule home.

****

Too devastated after losing Jim Guy and lacking the words to express her feelings, Angela began painting again. She switched from idyllic landscapes to the farm's core: animals and field workers. She often focused on hands, saying, "Hands reflect people by the knots and scars they accumulate."

After she had used the molly to pull the tractor upright, she never again harnessed or even drew that mule in harness. The image of Jim Guy's lifeless body lying in the dirt cut too deep. Now she painted that mule, her gray muzzle buried in grass, browsing next to Pansy, the milk cow. A mismatched pair, they were an odd couple, seemingly content to be near each other.

She sketched Bugle sleeping on the porch, drew cats pinned-wheeled around their morning milk, or crows perched on a fence post so real they could be seen cawing and pumping up and down. Those things held the essence of the farm for her, its sweat and struggle.

Chapter 17
Reconnection

May 1967

Unable to understand the "teach-ins" at colleges and universities or line up behind those that spoke against the war, Reid entered Clemson and disappeared into his studies. He ached, remembered arguments with his sister, his classmates, and his friends. Arguments that fell along the stop-communism-domino-war theory. By his last semester, although ambivalent, Reid enlisted in the Marines Corps.

The recruiter grabbed the signed induction papers before Reid replaced the cap on the ballpoint, promising him prime duty, training of his choice, and a 90-day deferred entry program.

Too late, Reid realized he had signed a contract for his soul with Old Scratch.

****

"Oh my gosh—it's Reid Davis Holcombe."

Reid whipped around at the sound of that creamy drawl despite the lunch hour din.

"Holy morning glory. My favorite bookworm." He smiled and repositioned his food tray. The college cafeteria swirled as he watched Ellie sashay toward him. He held the tray with one hand, extended the other to her, palm open. "As I live and breathe, the incomparable Eleanor Smythe. I thought you and all the other ladies wanted a women's only college experience. Last time I saw you, you were absorbed in that French woman's book. Seemed racy." He grinned, raised a wicked eyebrow, and guided her to the edge of the dining maelstrom.

"Yeah." She flashed a smile and floated along with him. "Simone de Beauvoir's book, *The Second Sex.* I jumped back and forth between her and Virginia Woolf," Ellie said.

"Woolf? What the sweet hell did she write?"

"*A Room of Her Own.*"

"That your plan for getting married? Have your own room?"

Ellie laughed. "Could be," she said, "but I read other things too."

"Like what?" Reid said.

"Ernest Hemingway."

"Wasn't he sexist? A man's man. They don't seem to go together."

"Well, if you consider Martha Gellhorn, it fits."

"Gellhorn?"

"The journalist. Hemingway's third wife. I read her stuff too. She stayed with her one true love," Ellie said.

"Old Ernie? Papa?"

"No, not him. Journalism. Her writing. She was addicted to wartime excitement, a regular junkie. Let's not talk about me. What's happened to you?"

The din of students moving along the serving line, chairs scraping across the floor, and friends shouting across the room grew deafening. Odors of frying hamburgers and raw onions, the clank of ice in glasses, and banging of grease-coated trays suggested hysterical order.

"Are you getting lunch or what?" He jiggled his tray.

"Yeah, sure."

"Let's find a place to sit where we can talk." He motioned with his head to the outside.

She glanced across the cafeteria, its mayhem of bodies, and signaled okay. He shifted toward the double glass doors leading outside.

"I'll get something and meet you." Ellie stepped into the serving line, grabbed a tray, selected utensils, and slid toward the salads and desserts.

In high school, during his junior and senior years, Reid had been passionate about Ellie while she ran hot and cold. She'd dated him, smothered him in unbridled lust, and then grow icy, abruptly withdrawing into the labyrinth of the women's basketball team. Not until she and Grace McCarthy linked arms and waltzed off together on a scholarship to Wellesley, did he figure it out.

He glanced up in time to see Ellie balance her tray in one hand, pull the door open, and step outside. Sunlight filtered through her skirt, offering a gauzy outline of her hips and legs.

They sat beyond the clatter of students and plates, ate, and talked. A reluctant breeze kept the odors of cooked sauerkraut and grilled hot dogs at bay. Paper napkins blew across the commons.

Ellie tucked an errant kink of red hair behind her ear, arranged the food, and picked up her fork. "What are you doing here?"

"Studying business marketing but Uncle Sugar needs me in Vietnam," Reid said. "I've got a ninety-day deferred plan, and then I'm all Marine. Can you believe the rotten luck?"

"Rotten luck? Didn't you volunteer?"

"Yeah. But I'm leaving and you just got here. That's rotten." He shook his head. "When did you decide to be a Tiger?" He munched on a carrot stick and watched her.

She took a bite of salad, chewed, and swallowed. "I tried Wellesley for six semesters. Loved it but wanted to see how you jock-types live. Besides, I can't give up on the man who gagged dissecting our lab frog. We almost failed that class."

He reared back, balanced the chair on two legs, and guffawed. "Uh-oh, girl. I do remember that. We needed the credit to graduate high school. Can you believe I had such a puny stomach?" He laughed again and shook his head. "I asked you to marry me because you were so brave."

"Not because I was so hot?"

"Alas, pretty lady, you preferred 'the coed college experience as a single woman.' Isn't that what you said?" He thunked the chair down and propped his elbows on the table. "Of course, you went to an all-women's college, not exactly coed. What was that?"

"Wanted to get out of the South. See how others lived. Explore options."

His eyes widened. "You? You've lived so many places with your dad being a preacher."

"You said you wanted out of here too." She grinned, moved a tomato wedge around in her salad bowl, stabbed the chunk, and popped it in her mouth. Juice squirted out and dribbled down her chin, leaving a trail of seeds stuck to her blouse. "Oh drats."

Reid howled. "You learn that in Boston?"

"Oops," she said, slowly licked her lips, and wiped her mouth.

"You turn me on like no other female has ever done," he said. "Let's pick up where we left off. Marry me before I learn Uncle's best methods for destroying Asian cultures."

"Reid. Good grief. You do go on." She pushed her tray back and reached across the table to pet his mustache, a brushy chevron.

"Marry me. I've got to the end of the semester before I have to report." He held her hands and rubbed his whiskers across her fingers. "You've done your thing with women. Been north and all that. Clemson's your single coed gig. You stay here while I travel foreign lands. I come back, Uncle helps with graduate school, and we're set to rule the world."

"Marry?" Ellie stared at Reid. "Legally? Preacher and all that?"

"Church or JP. We can jump over the broomstick. Whatever you want." She folded her arms on the table and cocked her head to the side. "And your dad? Angela and Jim Guy? The farm?"

"Dad runs the tobacco. Angela and Jim Guy do the farming. Besides, they'll iron things out on their own. You and me can start our own dynasty of redheads. Live in the wilds of the mountains. Someplace, anyplace without tobacco."

Ellie pulled her hand free, tilted her head back, and smiled. "Dynasty of redheads. How's that going to work? You've got dark hair. Lord help, but you do go on."

"Damn right." He howled again.

The noise increased a decibel before tapering off as students finished lunch and rushed toward afternoon classes.

Ellie, still cackling, picked up her tray, and glided back through the doors into the cafeteria. Reid followed her, tray balanced in one hand, and continued chuckling.

Turning around, she snickered and flashed a smile. "On the other hand, I do love a good adventure."

"Great. We'll get married and you finish your degree while I tour the mystic Orient."

She placed her tray at the kitchen pass-through and paused. "Bless your heart, I think you're serious."

"Sweet hell, yeah, I'm serious. A man should never propose marriage, even in jest, to a woman drooling tomato pulp."

Chapter 18
Eleanor Holcombe, Boston

April 1967

When Ellie first arrived in Beantown with its great array of academics, history, and culture, she found people who rolled "e" into "a" or added "da" to phrases. Honey-smeared vowels and words with "er" tacked onto the end were no longer heard. People that spoke with a Midwestern twang or a musical lilt entered her world.

Ethnic enclaves with an array of foods spiced with cumin, cardamom, and black mustard expanded her low country trinity of onions, bell peppers, and celery. Live theater, author readings, music concerts, political speeches, and dance performances spread out before her, all available for weekly consumption.

People with their different hues, textures, and fashions captivated her. With no social group, no clique, and no expectations, she could introduce herself as Eleanor Smythe, focused, self-confident, and adventurous. She dressed and dated without regard to hometown status and social-ladder expectations. For the first time in her life, she invented and reinvented herself around her red hair, freckles, and tomboy attitude.

In her senior year, Carolina roots called. She transferred from Wellesley to Clemson and ran into

Reid again. An unexpected and troublesome thing.

If she married him, what changes could she tolerate?

Chapter 19
Reid Holcombe

March 1967

Years prior, in high school, Reid had carried the team to All State. A popular basketball star, he tagged Ellie as dateable. The ubiquitous covey of cheerleaders constantly surrounding him did not dissuade him.

Unlike many athletes, he earned good grades. His sister Angela helped him with math, but the history and English grades were his. A voracious reader, he consumed all things Roosevelt, the two world wars, and Korea. Surprisingly, he discussed his reading with his doddering history teacher and the debate team coach. Reid and his teachers were sometimes found in a library study carrel, heads bent over books and magazines, talking rapidly and gesturing.

This chance reconnection with Ellie scrambled Reid's decision to join the Marines. He knew what the gossips said: spoiled daughter of a preacher, willing to experiment with drugs, too politically liberal, and worst of all, an undecided sexual preference. No matter, he had an itch for her like he had for no other woman.

They drove north to Spartanburg one Thursday through a pouring rain. Reid had trouble seeing the road and more than once Ellie slammed her foot against an imaginary brake. They arrived after courthouse business hours; even the cleaning crew had left the building. They drove back to the highway and pulled into an all-night truck stop where they sat drinking coffee and talking, soaring on adrenaline, unable to rent a room on their student budget. They preferred to save for their honeymoon night.

By five the next morning, long haul truckers pulled off the road and allowed rush hour traffic to flow through while they had breakfast and slept a few hours. The eighteen-wheelers, like great teams of horses and wagons, lined up along the back-parking lot. Men swung out of the tractor cabs, left them still rumbling, stretched, and swayed toward the restaurant. They sat in booths, ordered black coffee, bacon, grits, and fried eggs. Eventually, brown toast and grease odors hung over the tables. A constant clanking of dishes rose and fell, marking time for the customers.

Ellie and Reid, with the night behind them, watched the drivers lumber in. The two lovers ordered their breakfast with juice, no more coffee. They ate and played footsie under the table until Ellie pushed herself away and dabbed at her mouth.

"This is my wedding day. Excuse me while I comb my hair and freshen up," she said.

Reid rose to escort her to the restrooms. She took his arm and they sashayed toward the rear hallway. He stopped to read the community bulletin board while she pushed into the dingy toilet, glancing in the flaking mirror, and wrinkling her nose at the mingled odors of bleach and urine.

When she came out, her groom-to-be stood next to the ice cream freezer and held up a plastic rose.

"Smell it. That cashier squirted perfume when I

told her we were getting married. It's your wedding bouquet."

Hours later, a craggy justice of the peace married them. He grinned and commented, "A pleasant way to start *my* day. Good luck with your marriage."

Several clerks tossed paper punch-holes at Reid and Ellie as they ran down the courthouse steps. Ellie stopped to toss her plastic wedding rose to the motley group, grabbed Reid's hand, and raced around the corner to his used mustang, its hood held closed with bailing wire.

They drove to historic downtown Rock Hill, along the Catawba River, and spent their honeymoon night in an older motel, not far from the quaint botanical Glencairn Gardens. Rather than eat, they skipped dinner that night, preferring to explore their new husband-wife status.

The scent of semen and sweat proved to be a powerful aphrodisiac.

****

Reid and Ellie didn't tell a soul until Tuesday when they went back to Clemson and their classes. By Friday, friends gathered in the Tiger Pub, cheered the couple with Miller beer and pretzels, and peppered them with lewd jokes before handing over a wedding gift of assorted condoms. Ellie laughed until she caught hiccups.

As they left the pub, a calico kitten sat under a car meowing, apparently lost. Reid, on hands and knees, scrambled around, managed to grab the scrawny creature, and, turning to Ellie, announced with a beery smile, "Your wedding gift. Our first family member."

Ellie squealed. The kitten, wet and smelly, meowed

louder. "Let's call her Second-Hand Rose because she's a little throwaway. That's the perfect name and it goes with our plastic rose."

Chapter 20
Holcombe In-Laws

March 1967

Angela had squared off against Ellie as soon as she found out Reid was interested. She had known Ellie during their high school years and viewed her as a flamboyant town princess dragging Reid away from the beloved farm. She railed against Ellie's enrollment in one of those Northern colleges where Catholics bred like rats and acted like lemmings behind the Pope.

Jim Guy tried to reason with Angela, but she refused his efforts, declining even to attend the requisite small-town wedding shower the local churchwomen threw after the fact.

With the marriage, the old man had grown sullen and silent, left the house and farm, and spent time at local cafes drinking coffee with his cronies or simply roaming up and down the country roads. He lashed out by spending the farm payments on yet another cow or tractor implement, usually creating a scene at the bank or feed store.

Late one Wednesday afternoon at the Winn-Dixie, the store manager was called to break up a shoving match between the old man and a Baptist deacon over a jar of smooth peanut butter. The old man had reached for the jar at the precise instant as the deacon. They both demanded *that* jar despite others lining the shelf.

Not wanting to back down, the old man, both hands around the jar, shouted and shoved until he fell against a cereal display blocking the entire aisle. He dropped the peanut butter jar and watched it roll away. The deacon grabbed for it, missed, leaned against the jelly shelf, and began to pray. Town gossips repeated accounts of the fracas, and speculation spread like fleas on a fat dog.

****

Ellie and Reid rented a nondescript house in Beaufort soon after he entered boot camp. She landed a job with the Chamber of Commerce. He completed boot, then specialized training, and shipped for Nam late-1966. Within a month after Reid left, Ellie's tummy rounded out and Angela became giddy with the idea of being an aunt.

Eight months into Reid's second tour, a tractor rolled on Jim Guy and killed him. Ellie stood by Angela through the community visitation, church service, and later, countless suffocating nights drinking coffee while they grieved.

Ellie had a knack for being there whenever the tobacco boys and large landowners came around offering to buy the property. She planted her feet in the doorway and gave them all a slice of attitude whenever they pressured Angela to sell or lease the place out.

In the end, Ellie had her problems too. She agonized over Reid's fate. Vietnam, after all, was a dangerous place, relentlessly devouring men. The idea of wearing her black dress yet another time in one year made her whimper.

Chapter 21
The Discharge

April 1970

The causeway over Archer's Creek shortened the drive from the farm to Parris Island and Port Royal. By comparison, after years of hurry-up-and-wait in the military, Reid's return to the civilian world happened fast. Shock, a sense of disconnect, and gut-deep confusion settled on him. Again.

Six years had dissolved since he marched down Panama Street into the entry portal at the Marine Corps Recruit Depot. During the Vietnam years, he and hundreds of other young men strode through the gates on yellow footprints into boot camp and later, specialized training. Many never returned. Those that came back, returned changed. Trying to understand any motivation was like explaining how water tastes.

****

Mustering-out paperwork revised and completed, Reid drove back across the bay toward Beaufort and Willington. Once across, he stopped and pulled off onto the shoulder.

Stepping out of the truck, he watched waves lap along the beach. Sunlight glittered on the wet sand. Shore birds scurried across low-tide mudflats and ripples eddied against their spindly legs. Out on the bay, whitecaps laughed toward the open ocean. He sucked in a breath, licked the briny feel off his lips, and stared into the distance.

He tapped out a cigarette, lit up, clicked the Zippo closed, and took a long, deep drag.

The in-and-out swish of the sea and squawks of gulls riding air drafts were peaceful. Sea oats grew sparse across the loose sand, bowed gently in the wind, then sprung upright in a noble fight to anchor the beach. The sun glided toward the horizon and began a fierce, glowing decent.

With his eyes closed in the dwindling light, images quivered before him: Camouflage shirts. Miniskirts. Ho Chi Minh sandals. *Quân* trousers. Black plastic bags.

From his first week in Vietnam, he had counted the days before he could leave and return to *The World*. Until *she* had appeared and complicated *everything*.

Good church people, pinstripe-suit politicians, military brass, and row-crop farmers had sent him to fight and preserve democracy. He lived on adrenaline so heavy he tasted it, stayed pumped up weeks at a time, followed by a crash into numbness. And guilt.

Semper fi—always faithful. Now, different.

Chapter 22
Blue Star Bar and Grill

April 1970

Reid pulled into the parking lot at the Blue Star Bar and Grill, knowing Eleanor would not be home until after six. Time enough for a few cold ones.

To Reid, beer joints had a sameness—weather-whipped buildings with potholes of standing water, oil shimmering on the surface. A ubiquitous collection of dented pickups splashed with pasture muck, panel trucks, and rusted Fords sat in the gravel lot. Sometimes, older model Buicks or Cadillacs reflecting better times, were parked near the door.

He switched off the ignition, got out, and strode into the Blue Star, relishing its watering hole familiarity. The dimness relaxed around him. Pungent body odors and cigarette smoke hovered visible. A neon sign buzzed. Vinyl stools lined the scuffed bar. Several pool tables squatted along the back while a jukebox sat against the wall near the toilet doors.

A weary barman sighed when he saw Reid and continued to wipe a spill with his stained cloth. Beer tap handles stood poised for a draw next to shelves of bottled courage. He ordered a beer, drained it in two tilts, and watched construction workers talk trash as they played pool, called pockets, and bet quarters. He ordered a second beer with whiskey back, lit another Camel off the butt, swiveled away from the bar, and moved toward the pool tables. He sat on a stool against the wall, tossed the whiskey back, sipped the beer, and watched the game.

A road crew, roughhousing, talking loudly, ordered Buds, and sat at the bar. After several rounds, a heavy-set man stood and sauntered over to Reid.

"Looks of you, I'd say you gotta be military. You been in Nam?"

Reid took a long swig of beer, pulled a final toke from his cigarette, and crushed it in a too-full ashtray before he swiveled around to face the man.

"Yeah. I been there."

The man grinned and hollered at his companions. "Told you. I can always spot them with that haircut." He waved at a kid in khakis and pivoted back to Reid. "Got my little brother with me. He's gonna want to hear this. Come on over here, kid."

A tanned fellow in khakis sauntered over, beer sweating in his hand. He snickered as he walked up and slapped his brother on the back.

"Nam? Rough over there?" the khakis-clad kid asked.

"I handled it. What did you do?"

"Never went. Deferred. College and all that."

"Yeah? Reid tilted his head, "Rough handling all those books?"

Khakis stared at him, brayed coarse without mirth, and gulped his beer, Adam's apple bobbing. "I kept my grades up. Did okay. You done any killing? I mean up close?"

"Yeah."

"No kidding? How many?"

They always asked the same thing—how many?
The question never ceased to annoy him. *Suppose he
said zero. No one—even those who were there—could
grasp the confusion, the personal terror of a firefight.
He always lied when asked that question. What did it
matter?*

He tapped out another cigarette, lit up, and closed
the lighter with a snap before he tossed back the
whiskey. He savored the familiar bite and drawled out
his answer, deliberately calculated to shock.

"I stopped counting after a dozen and a half." *That
usually shut them up.* Reid's scalp tingled.

"A dozen—and a half? What's the half?" the
heavy-set worker asked. He shifted his bulk and
glanced at his younger brother.

Khakis squinted at Reid. "A half?"

"A kid."

"That's cold—keeping count. And a kid too,"
Khakis snorted.

"Why'd you ask if you didn't want a number?"
Reid's voice carried a note of menace.

"Don't get me wrong. I don't love them people—
kinda wanted to know if you took care of any of the
bastards." The worker, face flushed, a beer sweating in
his hand, stomped away. His brother followed.

Reid watched them go.

Pool sticks slammed into cue balls, spinning stripes
against solids in staccato barks. A construction worker
put his cue away, scooped up his winnings, and
dropped a quarter in the jukebox. "We Gotta Get Outta
This Place" throbbed across the room. The man nodded
and settled onto a vinyl stool.

Reid acknowledged the gesture. He closed his eyes. Morning fog, tracer rounds, and the stink of rotting vegetation enveloped him. Elephant grass brushed his palm. He clenched his teeth against bone shattering concussive shocks.

He opened his eyes as a tall waitress minced by. He gestured toward the empty jigger and beer, "Another one." She popped her gum and signaled okay.

A shot of brown liquid materialized before him, a sweating beer beside it. Dimly aware of the waitress serving two Coors for new customers, he tossed the whiskey back in a single motion, allowed the oak-seasoned taste to dull the sounds, the sights, and the smells around him.

Questions somersaulted through his mind until he muttered under his breath—when did I turn mean? Why did I come back? He nursed his beer, toyed absently with the shot glass.

"What time is it? Ellie should be home." He spoke aloud, rubbed his temples, massaging the concentric shock waves that rippled through him.

He stood, wobbled the length of the room, steadied himself against the bar, and left a disorganized pile of bills. He swayed a minute, balanced against the corner, and lurched through the door into the heat and glare. The door banged close behind him.

Chapter 23
Áo Dào Woman

March 1970

Out on the highway, a car backfired, the sound diluted in late afternoon traffic. A motorcycle gunned pass, straight pipes screaming. An eighteen-wheeler decelerated, jake brakes chattering down. The heat became hot pins under a fingernail.

Reid's face glistened with sweat. He crouched and ran along the outside wall, veered to his left and dropped low, shielding his head with his arms.

A couple across the gravel lot stopped, gawked, and continued walking. A grizzled man circled and knelt an arm's length away.

"Hold on, buddy. You're home. Hold on a minute."

Face down, gravel ground into Reid's forehead and nose.

The stranger moved closer, placed a firm hand on Reid's shoulder, his fingers dug into the muscle. "We got 'em, buddy. We're safe. Point man took 'em out."

Reid glanced to either side and pushed his face back into the grit. He moved his tongue in and out of his mouth, the copper taste of blood hung in his nostrils. He lay still, breathing hard.

Somewhere in the lot, a hot engine ticked. Gravel crunched as a truck dieseled onto the asphalt. He trembled. Shadows quivered before him. He pulled himself to a crouch and spat.

"Yeah, man. I'm home. I'm okay. Sun got to me. I'm home." Beer curdled sour in his mouth. He rose, rubbed his eyes with his knuckles, and stumbled toward his pickup. "I'm okay now. Too much light. That's all. Too much light."

The stranger moved back, but continued to drone, "Point man wasted them. We're safe. We're home."

Reid sat in the pickup, eyes closed, and gripped the steering wheel until his knuckles turned white. He stared at the potholes glistening with oil and watched a woman walk toward him on a sugar-sand beach, barely beyond the ripple of waves. She wore a long tunic with side slits, an *áo dài*, and flowing *quan* trousers. She carefully stepped around the potholes; a braided rope of hair hung down her back. Through the window, she touched his face, hovered for a single breath, and dissolved.

"No sense going on. Gotta stop. Can't live like this." He opened the door, vomited into the gravel, closed the door, and sat, head resting on the steering wheel. Not until his shoulders spasmed from the strain, did he gather himself, turn the ignition over, and ease out of the parking lot.

Chapter 24
Le Thi Linh

February 1968

Still a small child during the Indochina occupation, Le Thi Linh had learned basic survival rules from the French soldiers. When Americans replaced the French, she learned new rules: Don't run when Americans come to the village; you'll get shot. GI's don't think it funny when you steal sunglasses or shoes. Age doesn't matter. Getting caught may mean getting passed from hand to calloused hand.

At ten, she gravitated toward the Communists. Often, she squatted on a hillside, under the pretense of watching water buffalo, as their lookout. From there she could give an early alarm against any soldiers—South Vietnamese or American—approaching the village. As she grew older, she moved north, trained as a medic in Hanoi, and learned to handle weapons.

By the time her body ripened, she was ordered south again and assigned to local clinics in the delta. There, she gathered information, disclosed troop movements to her contacts, and cared for damaged children.

When her parents died in their rice fields two years later, she placed a lotus blossom near their picture and wore a white head band, signaling her grief. However, when her husband, a North Vietnamese army regular had been killed in Hué during Têt, she grieved alone fearing ARVN spies or American spooks, too unsure of the political sympathies of those around her to openly grieve.

Reid, her enemy, gradually became her self-styled protector and unwitting informant. Once, when they had sat together eating gooey rice cakes, she cried and whispered to him in Vietnamese. He did not understand. He began to speak of taking her home when he left, his personal war prize, making his dreams, her dreams.

Chapter 25
Midnight

May 1970

The charcoal voice rasped. *I can't do it anymore. I have to go. I'll wait near the beach for you. Near that blue water.*

"Don't leave. Things will get better. We're home." Reid pressed his head against the doorframe.

The voice did not respond.

Drained, Reid lit a cigarette, smoked it down, and lit another off the butt. "Say okay. You understand? Say it!" He slid down the wall and slumped on the floor.

Silence.

"Goddamn you, say it."

Okay. A choked sob vibrated into the air.

He sat, waited to hear the repeated okay, then stood, and leaned against the door jam. Metallic smells and the odor of death rose his nostrils, caused his stomach to convulse. He swallowed and listened.

The house creaked and moaned like a dying thing. A screen banged on a windowsill near the back. A limb scratched against the wood siding.

Finally, he shifted toward the sink, made coffee, poured a cup, and sat outside on the porch. A watery light crept across the sky as another sweltering day developed.

Bugle trotted up the steps and sat next to him, occasionally shifting. A cow lowed, mournful and long, in the west pasture. The scent of mangos rose delicate and peach-like. He shivered, unable to control the pounding in his head, a personal soul-rot gnawing. Life surrounded him and pushed him forward.

No beginning, no end. Like Vietnam, with no front lines, no rear lines.

Chapter 26
Pigeons Triangle Neighborhood, Beaufort

April 1970

Reid understood home had a way of making a person carefree and crippled, lighthearted and angry, flipsides of the same coin.

Beaufort, one of South Carolina's oldest towns, typified the low country culture. Perched on Port Royal Island, it served as a gateway to the coastal Sea Islands, Old South antebellum tourist attractions, and the military-business-commercial complex.

Historic homes in the Pigeons Triangle neighborhood sagged along the run-down streets, vaguely resembling birds sitting on a wire. A few of the smaller, privately owned, one-story wooden structures juxtaposed against the worn rental units made the area a mixed fixer-up dream.

Preoccupied, he missed a turn and circled back into his old neighborhood. Seemed like a lifetime ago, he and Ellie had rented their first home in this run-down area. Now no longer decked out in peeling paint, their house was different with its bright colors and jumble of flowers surrounded by uncut grass. A buckled, cracked sidewalk still stretched in front.

Parking along the curb, he struggled to focus. Grover rose from the porch, ambled out to the street, lifted his leg, and squirted against the truck tire, leaving a wet streak on the black rubber.

The yellow mutt was still sniffing around when Ellie pulled in from work and found Reid leaning on the truck hood, smoking. Butts littered the ground near the tire.

Getting out, she slammed the station wagon door. Kinks of red hair frizzled around her face. Still dressed in a gray suit and low heels, she took a deep breath, and faced him.

Neighbors coming home from work glanced toward them before sauntering inside to their evening routines. Several boys rode bikes up and down the pockmarked street, talking trash with each other. Down the street a lawn mower started, an unmistakable sign of summer. A gelatin heat settled, and tree frog calls rose in shrill notes signaling courtship.

Ellie spoke, her voice non-committal. "I wondered when you'd be settled enough to come by—took five days. I wish you'd let me pick you up at the airport. We could have skipped the park. Now I've had too much time to think. What am I supposed to do? Kiss you? Get a lawyer? What?"

"Yeah. Whatever." He steadied himself on the truck, pushed off against the hood, and wobbled up the driveway. "Smile. I'm here now."

"Looks like you're feeling no pain. You stop off to drink some courage? Is that what it takes to face me?" She watched him negotiate his way forward.

"Maybe." He rubbed the back of his neck and rotated his shoulders, easing the tightness. Her slow rich voice sent shivers over him, made hair on his arms prickle up. Despite all the miles travelled, the different worlds, and sweat-stained nights, she was still his wife. He grinned, a rakish glint in his eyes.

"Angela called to let me know you were home," Ellie said. "I tried to get in touch with you. Never heard back. I started to drive out."

"Don't know as this place is home anymore. Not much left here for me."

"That's not true. Your roots, your memories are here. Generations of Holcombe's. Your sister's here." She watched his face and then added, "*I'm here.*"

"Memories? Generations?" He glared at her unfocused and rubbed his ear as if willing it to hear differently. "I got enough of that shit to fill a coffin."

"Damn, Reid. You come dragging in here, announcing you're home, saying let's talk, and then you throw up a brick wall and back away. What's that supposed to mean?"

He flipped the cigarette away and stood mute.

Grover sniffed around the station wagon and then sat at Ellie's side. A cat moseyed across the grass while a door slammed down the street.

"Diana will be here in an hour." Ellie's voice reverberated, sharp and clear. "She comes for dinner on Thursday nights. You need to meet her." She slipped car keys in her pocket.

"Diana? "Who the hell is Diana?" He stopped, put a hand on the station wagon taillight, and sorted through a confusion of names.

Ellie faced him. "A sometimes roommate. I wrote you. We work together on the Gullah Project. Along the Sea Islands. She's with the Chamber. Weekends, she ferries back to Beaufort. She spends her off-time here, splits part of the expenses. Since you left, it helps."

"Real accommodating." He swayed, rebalanced himself, stared down at his partially buttoned shirt, grime-encrusted fingernails, and glanced around the neighborhood. "What's a sometimes roommate?" He scratched at his chest.

The remnant sounds of homebound traffic floated among the houses. Window blinds at several houses parted as curious and prying eyes peered out.

"Good grief, Reid. It's been days since the park and now you show up like some returning Viking. You're drunk."

"I've only had one beer. One." He held up a finger emphasizing his point. "I'm not drunk." He slumped against the station wagon and yawned.

"Is that so? Only one? Well, you smell. In fact, you smell like some dive. Smoke, beer, sweat—the whole shebang."

"Sweet hell, Eleanor, I've been working the fields. Tobacco. You remember that don't you? Tar. Sweat. Dirt." He attempted to wipe his hands on his shirt and stared down at his boots. His voice rose a notch. "What do you plan to do with me now that I'm back?"

"What do you want me to do with you?"

Eyes narrowed, she watched him. He still had the hip roll of a pimp and a sleek swimmer's body. Add his muscular arms and he radiated animal physicality. A trickle of sweat slid between her breasts.

"You are still my wife."

"You are an egotistical prick or else blind. Maybe both," she said. "When you left for Nam, you declared a separation—non-binding were your words. You stopped writing. I did the best I could. Somewhere along the line, it all fell apart."

"I knew you didn't love me when we stood before that justice of the peace," he said.

"That's not true."

"You married me to cover up what you actually were."

"And what is that? Town punch? Slut? Lesbian? Wrong-side-of-the-tracks trash?" She hurled the words at him. "What?"

He shook his head, attempted to rattle his thoughts into order. "We never should have gotten married. We're too different."

"Seemed like a good idea at the time. Especially since there was no secret about what you were getting into. Besides, you were headed to Nam anyway," she said.

"Didn't expect you to get pregnant right away. That sort of changed things."

"We never discussed having a family, but I assumed you'd be pleased," she said.

"About what—knocking you up and leaving, or losing the baby?"

"Which one was more significant?"

"Doesn't matter now. Maybe we both lucked out." He staggered forward a step, caught himself, and stood swaying.

"Your old man still said you married down, especially since he wanted you—only you—to run the farm. He wanted you to marry a farm girl."

"Yeah, his way of controlling things. He misjudged. I never wanted the farm."

"I think he knew that, but it's all he had," she said.

"Angela was a farm girl. She actually wanted the farm. I should be grateful, her being the good daughter and all."

"He didn't consider Angela. Only you."

"Nope. Wasn't going to work that way." Reid readjusted to a more upright position.

Ellie set her purse on the vehicle hood, her voice quiet as a leaf settling. "I went to your dad's funeral."

"Yeah? How was that?"

She glanced down at the simple gold band on her left hand, her mind back at the open grave. Angela stoic in her black cotton dress, worn twice in the same year.

****

Months prior, Ellie had stood and held her sister-in-law's hand next to the old man's graveside while the preacher read from a scripture and intoned the usual earth-to-earth, ashes-to-ashes homily. Several couples from neighboring farms, Ollie Jacobson, three church ladies, and the Holcombe lawyer were the only white attendees. Neighbors filed by the grave, offered condolences, and hurried off to other obligations.

Mary and Calvin Terrell, in their Sunday best, had stood apart from the small collection with heads bowed, the last to leave.

Mary hugged Angela and spoke in her soft lilting patois. "I got nothing to say ain't already been said. But y'all know, you have a need, I be here." Mary moved to Ellie and patted her arm. "I'm here."

Calvin, at the foot of the grave, stooped, picked up a handful of dirt, and tossed it on the closed casket. He wiped his hands on a handkerchief and then shook hands with Angela before he shuffled to stand in front of Ellie.

Ellie extended her hand. Slow and deliberate, he inclined his head and shook. He replaced his hat, took

Mary's arm, guided her toward a dented '59 pickup, and held the door. She settled into the seat. Several cranks and the old vehicle coughed, caught, and smoked as they rattled away.

Arms linked, Ellie and Angela had walked over uneven ground to Ellie's station wagon, supporting each other.

****

Reid's voice tugged Ellie back to the present. She blinked several times and then answered. "Dignified. Graveside only. Angela told me she didn't know where you were. She sent a message through the Red Cross for you. Said she never heard back. At least, not from you."

"He was dead. No need to come. Besides, I had other obligations. There was a war on, remember?"

"And when Jim Guy was killed in that freak tractor accident? You could have come, at least for your sister. Was the war winding down then? Or were there *other* obligations?" Her voice had a scorched edge.

"Leave Sis out of it. She has enough grit in her craw to take on the whole damn tobacco industry. Didn't figure she needed me."

"She needed you. Still does. With everything disintegrating, she needs more than a sister-in-law and some hired help. More than church do-gooders and redneck neighbors speculating and gossiping. More than Big Tobacco suits circling like vultures, clutching their precious checkbooks."

He shoved his hands into his pockets and studied the street. Spanish moss dripped from limbs arched above the road. Modest houses, some well-groomed and others sliding into decay, stared back, silent as thought.

"I couldn't do it. I couldn't leave my men to come home for a *peaceful* funeral. Besides, that old man wanted to go."

"Death's not simple. Always losses and gains. Memories accumulate and you hand them along, one way or another."

"How would you know?" His voice cracked. "You have no idea about anything but those love-it-or-leave-it diatribes. As it turns out, no matter what the military and politicos told us, there were never any dominoes. No other countries lining up to be Communist."

Sweat dotted his upper lip. He clenched his teeth, the muscle in his jaw protruded from the force. He rubbed the bridge of his nose between thumb and forefinger.

"I tried. I tried hard to be a good wife." She frowned, toyed with her wedding band, and shook her head.

"When was that?" He leaned toward her, shouting until spittle flew. "The trying part. While I was in basic? Maybe when I got Westpac orders? Or re-upped? Tell me, when did you try?" His face glistened with sweat.

"You've got nerve. Real nerve talking to me like that." She stamped toward the house. Halfway across the yard, she stooped, picked up the evening paper, and continued. Grover trotted ahead, tail waving.

The porch groaned under her light step. She opened the screen door, held it with her hip, and paused. "I had a life separate from you. I was. . . *am* different. I think you always saw that. Even when we were in college."

"Damn it to hell, woman. You chased me down.

You married me." He jabbed his finger in her direction, his face contorted.

"Takes two. You have your own dark side. Besides, you got it wrong. *You* chased me down. Remember lunch?"

His voice cracked, shoulders sagged, and he shook his head. "Why me? Of all the swinging dicks around that prejudiced, hellforsaken, rat-hole college, why choose me?"

She unlocked the wooden door and flipped on the front room light. "Come back when we can *talk*. And *listen*." She stood framed against the door.

"We're still damn-well married. I haven't decided what to do about *that* little mistake."

"Neither have I." She closed the door.

Grover sat on the sagging steps, tongue lolling out. Two boys on bikes, stopped before the house, watched the argument a minute, and then rode on. Next door three girls squatted on the sidewalk playing jacks, occasionally squealing with delight. Across the street, an older woman ambled by carrying a bag of groceries.

Reid stalked down the drive and slumped chest down across the truck hood, arms flung wide. Finally, holding the side mirror, he stood, jerked the door open, and slid in. He pounded the steering wheel, cussed, cranked the truck, and yanked it into gear. Tires squealed as he pulled away from the curb. He rested his elbow out the open window, blinked repeatedly, and continued to cuss.

Birds flitted from one tree to another, their songs rising and falling, the only welcome home music Reid would hear in the hot afternoon.

"How can I love two different women? How? Both

want something else, something more than me." Air snatched his words and scattered them down the street.

Chapter 27
Discussion

March 1969

With a hand spade, Ellie dug holes in the flowerbed while Diana nestled purple pansies into the indentions and carefully tamped the soil around them. Ellie favored these petite spring harbingers, citing their yellow faces and resilience since they grew even if frost covered the beds.

"Remember Thanksgiving when Angela and I sat outside?" Diana paused in her planting, hands dangling open. "She told me she called her father the Old Man not out of tenderness but because he favored Reid. She even said she actually married Jim Guy to show her father she intended to stay and farm."

"She may have, but I also think she genuinely loved Jim Guy. I think he loved her, too." Ellie paused and reached for another container of pansies. "He was good *to* her and *for* her. He validated her as a person."

"She may have loved Jim Guy, but it was her dad she tried hardest to *please*."

"That's right." Ellie dug a hole and began settling the flowers. "I think he saw her as simply another big-hipped farmwoman. A worker. In fact, I think the old codger was relieved she married. He no longer had to be responsible for her."

"So much for fatherly love."

"Angela's a math wizard. And a watercolorist. Get her to show you some of her pieces."

Diana rocked back on her heels, hands propped on her knees. "I didn't realize that."

"She played volleyball in high school. I think the school even got a few trophies while she was on the team."

"Seems like an odd combination—math, volleyball, and watercolors."

Ellie filled the watering can and set it nearby, slipped her gloves off, and brushed at dirt stains on her knees. "She teaches middle school math and covers some of the coaching for girls' volleyball and basketball."

Diana settled another plant into a hole. She stood and grimaced as she straightened her back.

"I was surprised the first time I realized Angela did watercolors. The things you find out after you get married." Ellie snorted at herself and began to water the flowers.

Diana plopped down in a patio chair with the cat and listened.

"Once she found out I was pregnant, she warmed up. That's when she first mentioned her art. Occasionally, she'd invite me to go while she did field sketches. Going out like that with her, I realized how much fun she was. And how deeply family mattered to her."

"She told me Reid defied his dad by taking off for Clemson the year after he graduated. He farmed that first year, wanted no more, and took off to get a business degree. Worked his way through college with the usual hodgepodge jobs."

"Everything Reid did seem to be a reaction, not a choice." Ellie slipped her gloves on and stooped again to planting.

"You included?"

"Especially me. His father called me town princess, white punch, snob—said I'd never make a farm wife, that I'd drag Reid into the city, waste his talent. Let the farm deteriorate. I think he married me to double down on his dad." She snorted and shook her head, crab-walked to another section of the flowerbed and continued planting.

"Oh? Not because you were so hot? Or pregnant?"

Ellie burst out laughing. "I'll admit we had some grand times creaking those bedsprings. But truth be told, I didn't know I was pregnant at the time. He shipped in '67 and I found out after he left. I wrote, thinking that would make him happy. Give him a reason to come home."

"Did it?"

"He wrote sometimes. Mentioned the baby once. I think it confused him. I tried to visualize what he must have been going through. Tried to understand."

"What happened when you miscarried?"

"I wrote. Told him I lost the baby and was super depressed. He said it was not a good time for a baby anyway. I couldn't figure out if he was relieved or trying to ease my disappointment and hurt. That was one of the times he signed his letter 'with love.' After that, he signed 'devotedly' until they dried up. I sort of dissolved for him." Ellie smiled and glanced at Diana. "Dissolved for myself too—until you came along."

"So, I'm the rebound affair."

"No. Of course not. You're a part of myself I never allowed to fully surface. Only thought about."

"So, what do you want now?"

"I don't know." Ellie stopped, shucked her gloves, and picked at the dirt, crumbled several hard clumps. "I feel scuffed around. Used. With you here, I find myself shifting, changing. I think about relationships and careers differently. I want you. I'm not sure I want him home anymore."

Diana listened, her hand lightly scratching the cat around the ears.

"I'm attached to the Gullah project," Ellie said, "and can't image it without us together. You know, working as a team. Do you realize we sometimes actually finish each other's sentences?"

The entire backyard, albeit dressed in March brown, reflected a cross between seasonal confidence and humid afternoons spent pulling weeds. Both women were silent a few minutes. Grover lay dozing in the sun, his day peaceful. Rosie purred.

Ellie rocked back, her hands draped on her knees, spade dangling loose. "Don't think I ever told you, but when we were in high school, I ran for student council president. After my speech, Reid stood and clapped—only him. Everyone else sat and stared. Bell rung about that time and the assembly let out."

"Did you win?"

"No. Maybe that was a sign." She began collecting her gloves and gardening tools, piling them into an empty bucket.

Diana rose from the chair, sat Rosie aside, and put her hand on Ellie's arm. "Honey, you sound like you still love him." She dropped her hand. "You'll

127

eventually have to decide between me and him. You've also got to think long term. About your career. Time to choose is just around the corner."

"Yes, I know. I want both of you. I want the career, too." Ellie rolled her eyes. "Simply put, I want it all."

"It's not going to work that way," Diana said. "I'll not share. I may be part of the new woman movement, but I'm still old fashioned enough to be monogamous. I'll only share the career thing."

Ellie moved away from Diana. "Damn it all, he and I need to talk first. I want to hear how he feels." She shook her head and put a bag of topsoil in a rusted wheelbarrow. "Besides, you know how people are. Especially here with this small-town mentality. Even if Reid and I divorce, we can't keep the reasons quiet."

"Am I the backup plan if he doesn't want you anymore?"

Ellie's face wrinkled into a frown. "Of course not. But I—well, I need to talk with him. I can't throw in the towel until we talk. I owe him that. *He* owes me."

"I have a good career. I make solid money and stay on the move. I like being independent, like making my own decisions. I like moving and not fighting the establishment quite the same."

"But you don't have family, no roots. I grew up that way and I'm not sure I want that again."

"Either you and I are together or we're not."

Ellie turned, faced Diana, her words sharp. "Are you saying I tag along behind you, give Reid up no matter what he says?"

"I'll not throw away my work, my career. Something has to happen," Diana replied. "Besides, if you go with me, you'll not have to worry with community reaction and protecting reputation. As contractors, we'll move every few years."

"I have an obligation to Angela and Reid. I can't leave them in disgrace."

"Family loyalty, is that it? And what about me?"

"You understood what my situation was *before* we got involved." Ellie frowned, stood up, stretched, and dropped the hand spade in the wheelbarrow.

"You knew about me, too."

They stared at each other, lips pursed.

"Knowing something in your *head* and knowing something on a *gut level* are two different things," Diana said.

"Okay already," Ellie said. "Reid's one helluva of a stud. He touches me—any place—I go from dry to wet like that." She snapped her fingers. "I wonder if it'll be the same when he gets home."

"And with me?" Diana glared, her eyes narrowing into hard slits.

Ellie looked at Diana a moment, then smiled, wiggled her hips, and blew an air kiss. "Our relationship's different, more equal. Simpatico. You're delicious, like a sun ripened strawberry, meant to be savored. Sweet tart, that's you. A leisurely, warm spread." She licked her lips.

"You're wicked." Diana mimicked the kiss, reached for Ellie's hand. "Delicious, huh? Love it." Lines around Diana's eyes deepened, became furrowed. She spoke slow. "It might be delicious, but it's close to decision time. For *both* of us."

"Let's not talk about that right now," Ellie said. She turned away. "I'm hungry. There's leftover chicken salad in the refrig. I think there's still some potato chips too. Come on." She knocked dirt off her garden boots, opened the screen door, and disappeared inside.

Diana collected the empty plant containers and threw them in the trash before she gathered the tools and wheelbarrow. By the time she got to the kitchen, Ellie had washed her hands, pulled the chicken salad out, opened a loaf of bread, and ripped off paper towels. She stood rummaging in the refrigerator for mayonnaise.

Diana grabbed plates and put them on the kitchen counter, bumping Ellie with her elbow.

A pretend pout playing on her face, Ellie bumped Diana back. They fell to giggling, bumping, and making sandwiches. Diana popped a beer, took a long swallow, and gestured sharing toward Ellie.

Feelings hovered between them, omnipresent, not quite disappearing, yet not quite distinct. They ate and shared the beer, opened another one, and drank it together. They finished, left the dishes in the sink, popped two more beers, and shucked their clothes, piece by piece, on the way to the bedroom.

"Strawberries for dessert!"

Chapter 28
Night Call

May 1970

With the June tourist season already full blown, pressure to finish the project report and the accompanying brochures, increased.

Wednesday night, Ellie brought rough drafts home, skipped her dinner, and revised late into the evening. Focused on the edits, she jumped at the sound of the phone ringing and scrambled to keep her stacks in order. Papers, balanced on the edge of the table, began a slow slide toward the floor. Ellie reached for them and missed, her pen smearing across several pages. A dark line marred three sheets. She groused under her breath and picked up the phone.

"Eleanor Holcombe? Mrs. Reid Holcombe?"

She did not recognize the male voice. "Yes. Who is this?"

"Deputy Kyle Mason, Colleton County Sheriff Department."

"Oh." She leaned back and stared at the phone as if a person might appear standing on the receiver. "Well, yes, I'm Ellie, Reid Holcombe's wife."

"He's in jail and asked that I phone you. I don't normally make these calls, but he and I went to Clemson together, served in ROTC there. I'm doing this as a personal favor, kind of on the side."

"Okay." Ellie gripped the phone, drew her question out slow. "Is there trouble?"

"Well, ma'am, he was driving erratically, got stopped, and ended up in a bit of an altercation with the arresting officer. He's been charged with resisting arrest and drunk driving. Since it was mostly verbal, I got it talked down to drunk driving."

"Oh, no." Ellie fumbled again, knocked a stack of graphics to the floor, and stared at the clock. Almost eleven. Not a good sign.

"He's living with his sister. Why didn't he call her?"

"I'm not sure. He mumbled maybe he had tapped her out. Besides, he said you would understand. He said call you since you were in Beaufort. Says he's too well known around here."

She grimaced. "What should I do? Come get him?"

"Well, we usually recommend giving a person time to sleep it off. And think. Better to pick him up tomorrow morning. You might aim for some time after ten."

Ellie stared at the scattered papers, grew frantic at the pending work, and silently blamed Reid. "Oh, hell," she said.

"You'll need to bring cash if you want to post bail."

"Double hell."

****

Reid stared at the ceiling, listened to the scuffing and trash talk of those in the holding tank, and became nauseous with the odors of human urine and unwashed bodies. A half-light bathed the concrete walls. Often, in

Nam, he had sat beside the concertina wire boundary of the firebase and watched fog dissolve. Night creatures crept away, seeking a protected spot to spend the day. Mosquitos, the only entities apparently unaffected by the war, swarmed around him.

More than once an empty whiskey bottle lay nearby with him hurling and unable to recall the previous evening.

Inside the perimeter during the dry season, dust swirled with the rising sun. Dirt beads accumulated in his neck creases, grit seeped into clothing, and irritated his crotch. Choppers, arriving and departing one, exacerbated the dirt. When the monsoons arrived months later, they brought rain pellets that stung whatever they struck, and the complex morphed into a quagmire.

At times in the field, light became translucent and the rice paddies stretched as green and endless as the sea. Sweat soaked his shirt, plastered it to his body. A random breeze would cause goose bumps to pop up along his arms, slightly cool him, and die, allowing the suffocating temperature to shoot up until his head throbbed.

Vietnam took on varied colors when the sunlight broke through the mist and dappled surreal shapes on the trail. Those times, he had been pulled back to Carolina picnics, summer watermelons, and the smell of fresh mown grass.

****

The jail gates banged open, a rude and jolting fingernails-on-a-chalkboard grate against his eardrums. The metal sound jerked him back to the present. From above, he stared at himself sitting in the drunk holding tank, his shirt opened against the swelter, tongue coated with a foul taste.

"Come on, Holcombe. Your wife's here. Don't know why she did it, but she's gone your bail."

He rose from his hip-squat against the wall and stepped forward expressionless.

Chapter 29
Angela Holcombe

June 1970

Every few weeks, between midnight and three, Angela listened as Reid talked to someone he apparently knew from Vietnam. The calls ended with a demand that the caller repeat "okay" several times. Like a promise or pledge.

The conversations, Reid's refusal to live with Ellie, and his broodiness confused Angela, made her days oppressive. She recognized he was not there, but off some other distant place. She missed Jim Guy, ached from the lack of his touch, her inner core swiveling without his presence. She *needed* both of her men.

****

A slight harelip made Jim Guy shy as a boy and caused others to look through him even as he grew to manhood, a shadow person. Plainly, he loved Angela, loved her years before they got married. They graduated high school together, rented a place in Columbia, and enrolled at the University of South Carolina becoming avid Gamecocks. They married within two months of their move. With a high lottery number, Jim Guy threw himself into his studies and later, after graduation, his work on the Holcombe farm. Angela relished the idea of being a farmer's wife. Until the day the tractor rolled over and Jim Guy was gone.

****

Alone, even with Reid home and Ellie living nearby, Angela marveled she didn't lose her mind, start running up and down the tobacco rows stark-naked. Maybe screaming too. After Jim Guy's death, she realized she was rationing out minutes of concern, locking her heart, leaking colorless liquids instead of love, and acting the miser.

Strangest thing, she didn't hear the phone ring anymore. She would simply wake up and hear Reid talking.

Chapter 30
Joe Terrell

April 1970

Rebuilding the barn brought one difficulty after another. Calvin accumulated enough boards for the initial job, but as Joe completed one section of the aging structure, he uncovered additional rotten wood that threatened collapse.

By late afternoon, with the rafters and supports stabilized, he stopped work and gimped down to the hog pen, the heat of the day barely dissipating. Pretty Sal trailed him. An insect chorus rose to a high C, slid off, and then rose again. He leaned on the fence, wiped sweat from his face, and watched the sow root around the edge of the pen. Ten piglets, shaded by a corner oak, slept in a jumble. He laughed aloud. His pleasure in watching the animals took his mind off the heat and chores.

At the sound of his father crunching along the path, Joe stepped away from the fence. The older man, his once broad chest curving inward and his frame gaunt, shuffled up. Worrisome signs to Joe.

"What's up, Pappy?"

"Son, I need hog feed, some them Purina pellets. Slow's I am, that feed store close before I can get there. You more spry than my old bones. You run by?"

"Store close at six?"

"Yeah," Calvin said. "It best to be there 'round 5:30 when them white folks anxious to close up and get home. They not as apt to nitpick over things. Especially you peel off green folding stuff."

Joe glanced down at his watch—a Seiko he brought back like many returning soldiers, his only luxury. "I think I can make it okay," he said.

"Might as well get coupla sacks of All Stock for the cow while you there. I let things get downright low. Guess I forgot."

"That's not like you." Joe frowned; worry nudged against him.

"Oh, I reckon things piling up too fast. Besides, I like to keep my time in town cut back." Calvin propped his backside against the fence and rubbed his hands together.

"You working under the 'don't see you, don't think about you' notion?" Joe chuckled and shook his head. He watched his pappy stare off across the barnyard. They stood silent, listened to the hum of life around them.

Joe spoke softly, as if thinking out loud. "Truth be told, Pappy, I thought that mixed-up mess of a war was my way out, way to see more of the world. I come back, discovered things the same. Only thing that changed is me. Now here I am wanting and expecting more'n than I'm getting. I think even them white boys come back changed. Not always for the better. Just changed."

Calvin brushed absent-minded at the gnats and stood watching his son. He nodded. "Changes coming should've been made long time back."

The piglets scrambled up and fooled around the sow. She snuffed, tilted her head up to Calvin, and grunted for a handout. Hog musk wafted up. A sassy jay perched above the pen, hopped to several different branches then flew away. In the distance, a crow cawed.

"You still got credit there?" Joe rubbed his hands together.

"At that feed store? Naw. That old white man Shipman cut me off."

"When did that happen?" Joe's face scrunched; his brow knitted into worry lines.

"Jim Guy got that accident then Old Holcombe died. Miss Angela hired me cause she couldn't handle that farm alone. She says to Shipman let me have credit at the store. First, he says okay, but it upset folks herebouts when word got out him giving credit to likes of us."

"I understand the black part but why against Miss Angela?" Joe shifted from the fence, stood square, and studied his pappy's face.

"Them tobacco boys gots an eye on that Holcombe place. They figure they get to anyone that hep them. Make them quit so Miss Angela have to sell out. Besides, white trash don't want black folks to have stuff. Even if it's only credit. Shipman say Miss Angela don't tell him how to handle his store especially when it come to us people. Says no more cuff. Cash only. Says she too soft on our kind anyway." Calvin massaged his gnarled hands, shook his head, and grew thoughtful.

Joe bristled. "That word 'uppity' came up pretty often too, don't it?"

"Well, yeah, but them white folks can't hardly talk 'out *somebody* hollering uppity. Your mamma and me get by. Right now, you go with the flow."

"Damn it all to hell and back. I didn't go all the way to Nam and come home to live in this racist muck. I'm a man." Joe gestured at the farm. "I've got my pride. We both have."

"I know son. For now, let's plow a straight row and be thankful we gots the plow. Things work themselves out. Take this here folding money and go on. Get that feed." Calvin thrust a small wad of bills into Joe's hands.

"It ain't right. We pull our own weight. All we're asking is fair treatment." Joe glared at his father, handed the bills back, "I got folding stuff. I use mine. We share."

Calvin leveled his hand at Joe; irritation crept into his voice. "Son, now you listen here. You leaving. You going north. Your mamma and me, we staying. We got our pride too. We gots to live here, so for now, we handle things our way. We know how to sidestep these people. Hear me? Go on. Get that feed and keep a civil tongue in you head."

Chapter 31
Reid Holcombe

June 1970

Most nights Reid slept restless. He chain-smoked and watched a woman's naked form hover in the shadows. He smelled incense. Groaning, he tossed the sheets aside and began to worry his balls.

She floated out of reach, her skin translucent. Not Ellie, not anyone. He jacked off and relaxed at the relief, his penis withering back into the tangle of pubic hair. He tossed the sheets further back and lay remembering things lost, things never to be reclaimed. He smelled the sea, saw shades of green.

He sat on the edge of the bed and thought of Ellie—her sassiness, fondness for animals, and her complex mixture of experiences. As a preacher's kid, her frequent moves made for shallow roots. Willington and Beaufort were the closest to a forever home she had ever known. His choosing to stay with Angela in his childhood bedroom threatened those tenuous roots, her sense of belonging.

He stood beside the bed, shivered, and listened as night sounds exacerbated the darkness. Ghosts in black pajamas beckoned. Men in green camouflage waited nearby, cussed, played cards, and drank beer. A headache bloomed jagged behind his eyes.

Reid sweated, dressed quietly and still breathing heavy, stood outside. It was safer in the shadows, away from the next grenade, from tracers carving up the blackness, and blood indiscriminately splattered when he stood too near.

Bugle rose from the porch, stretched, and trotted beside him as he walked toward the barns. When he paused, she leaned against his feet, grounding him with her shoulder and canine loyalty. She scouted ahead when he continued his rounds, security trotting with her.

An owl's mournful note floated into the dark. Reid cocked his head at the sound, wondering if it was the same owl of his youth. He craned his neck up, touched the rough tree bark, and waited for the mortars to fade and his trembling to stop. Flares stitched tobacco fields and rice paddies together in shades of orange light. Salt waves crashed against both shores. The owl called again, then lifted from the tree fork, and soared into tangled shadows spread across the fields. A woman's hand stroked his face. He sucked in his breath.

He and Bugle moved through dew-soaked grass, leaving a trail to the two-story barn. He checked for any errant heater that could smoke the leaves black or cook them too dry

He didn't fear Communism nor detest the war like friends that stayed home protesting. He needed to go, good or bad, a sure ticket off the farm, his passport to adventure, and another life. At least, he had planned it that way before he shipped.

Then Ellie reappeared with her red hair, small breasts, and infectious laugh.

They hiked, debated with friends, read, talked, and

laughed. They moved within rhythms colored by their moods. Their days melded together until he didn't remember why he married her—nor how he could survive without her.

Later, he questioned himself: when did he learn to relish the patrols, field highs, and the adrenaline rush?

A revolver bought from a pawnshop was solid and dangerous. He respected the feel of it. At night, he fondled it, checked the load, and slid it under his pillow. Maybe tomorrow.

Chapter 32
Bank Visit

July 1970

Reid dropped by the bank on Tuesday afternoon with as much of the farm back payment as he could scrape together. Vivian, the teller, blushed crimson when she recognized him. She fumbled filling out the receipt and dropped her pen twice.

"Didn't mean to create a difficulty bringing in cash. Only a partial payment at that." He smiled at her.

She barely glanced up. "It's no problem. Really. Thank you, Mr. Holcombe, for the payment. Do you realize you still have a balance?" She slid the receipt across the counter.

"Mr. Holcombe? Hell, Vivian, we went to high school together. Sure, that was a long time ago and we've both gotten older, but when do friends call each other Mr.?"

"Well, I'm at work now. I have to be formal." She glanced up at him, and then looked down.

"What happened to the hometown feel and friendly service this bank likes to tout?"

She paused, glanced down at her class ring, and offered a smile, albeit wafer-thin. "I'm glad you made it home. Angela kept me posted whenever she came in. We always tried to talk a minute whenever she left a payment. How is she?"

"Fine. And, to answer your question, I do realize there is an outstanding balance." Reid picked up the slip, studied her face, and asked, "Bank manager in this afternoon?"

"That would be Harvey Cavanaugh." Vivian's hand paused before she buzzed his office. She mumbled a response, took a deep breath, and said, "Mr. Cavanaugh will be out in a minute. There are some chairs over there where you can wait." She gestured to an alcove at the end of several glass-paneled offices. "He said to tell you please wait. You and he need to discuss your loan."

"Yeah. I'll bet." Under his breath, he repeated his mantra when walking point: tread careful, watch the shadows before you move, do everything slow, trust your instincts. You're alone. Danger's always present, even in a U.S. bank, especially when farm payments are behind. Sweat formed half-moon circles under his arms.

He stood next to the customer kiosk. After a few minutes, Cavanagh strode out, an unlit cigar sloppy between his teeth, spotted Reid and extended his hand in an obligatory gesture. They made safe small talk about the weather while he guided Reid to an enclosed conference room off the foyer.

The banker placed the cigar in an ashtray, opened a low credenza, picked up a bottle of Knob Hill, and gestured toward Reid. Without waiting for an answer, he poured two fingers of whiskey in separate glasses and set one before Reid.

"Good to see you home again," Cavanagh said. "Glad you made it back. I've heard things staying pretty rough over there."

"Yeah, pretty rough."

"Well, you men seem to be holding them Commies feet to the fire."

"That what you call it?"

"What would you call it?"

"Making the world safe for tobacco sales."

Cavanagh barely smiled and shifted, sweat breaking out on his forehead. "Guess that works over there. Stuff falling apart over here."

"Like what?"

"Well, it's been all over the news—Johnson not running for a second term, riots up north and out in L.A. Body bags coming back. Nixon. Everything going to hell."

"Angela tells me even the women are getting out of line."

Cavanagh chuckled, pulled out a handkerchief and mopped his face. "I'm sure you've been updated on all this. Not much we can do so long as President Johnson doesn't rein in the Negroes."

"Exactly what does that mean?"

Cavanaugh stared, his brow knitted in puzzlement and stuffed the handkerchief in his pocket. "All that Alabama stuff. Selma. Pettus Bridge. Johnson knuckling under with that voting bill. Guess you probably not keeping up with the news, what with your being gone and all." He picked up the cigar and rolled it between his fingers, cleared his throat and said, "Let's talk about what you came here for—your farm, your loan."

Reid's eyes narrowed to thin slits.

"You and your sister have had rotten luck what with your daddy and Jim Guy gone the same year.

Especially with you off in Nam. I was sorry to hear all that. My sympathies to you and Angela. Your wife too. You are still married, aren't you?"

Reid did not respond. He swirled whiskey around in the glass.

The banker mirrored the gesture. "Your sister missed a bank payment or two sometime around when Jim Guy had that accident. Then when your father died, she missed several more. Damn shame. My sympathy again. But I think we'll get it all fixed up."

"How's that? The fixed-up part?"

"Feds want to end the quota system, so tobacco buyouts have started." Cavanagh gestured with his cigar and continued. "Some of the big farmers and agribusiness are buying out the small farmers. They're wanting to consolidate the farms, cut costs, increase efficiency. A rep from R.J. Reynolds came by asking which farmers were floundering. They're expecting to pick up the note on some of those farms. They want to take the note straight from the bank. Some of the little farmers are selling. Some want to keep growing, so they are leasing their acreage back on share."

"And what does this have to do with our note?"

Cavanaugh shifted and leaned forward. "Your land is still profitable, and you still hold an allotment. I told those folks you'd had a run of bad luck. What with you being a war vet, they're willing to put a generous offer on the table. Help put you back on firm financial ground."

Reid frowned. "In other words, you want me—Angela and me—to sell the place. You're their stalking horse. Their Judas goat. That farm's been Holcombe for three generations." He watched the banker place his cigar on the ashtray.

Cavanaugh sat moment, picked his cigar up, thumped it on the ashtray. "You planning to farm?" He glared and rolled the cigar between forefinger and thumb, then replaced it again on the edge of the ashtray. "Didn't think you wanted to get your hands in that tar."

"Have you talked to Angela?"

"Well, Mr. Holcombe, you understand how women are, they don't see the business side of things. Everything seems to work better when men make the decisions."

"I guess that means she turned you down." Reid's mouth settled into a hard line.

Cavanaugh glanced down at the cigar, sipped his drink, and continued in a tense voice. "That farm's overburdened with debt and missed payments. Seems things are delicate for y'all right now. Especially since this mess landed on you right when you're getting back from Nam. Your credit's gone and with harvest and market season on us...well, it's got to be tough." Cavanaugh tapped his fingers on the table. "And, yes, I did talk with her and put an offer on the table."

"Friend of mine said you Suits, you men that dress clean every day, along with agri-company greed, is a big chunk of the country's problems. He might have been right."

"Now Reid, that's a little harsh don't you think? Here I am trying to help you get out of the hole and you're blaming me and the very people that can get you out of this mess. What kind of talk is that?"

"Actually no, I don't think it harsh. Getting your legs blown off. Taking shrapnel through the gut. Coming home in a body bag. That's harsh."

The man blanched. "Let's not get too graphic here."

"How much pain can you stand, Mr. Banker? How much morphine would help you? Know anything about that?" Reid's voice carried a note of menace.

"Am I to assume you're threatening me?"

Reid picked up his glass, stared at the liquid, and took a sip. "You've got some good Tennessee water here." He placed the monogramed glass on the table with a sharp clink.

Cavanaugh cleared his throat. "Bank management won't tolerate any more missed payments. They'll foreclose if you are even so much as late." He leaned forward, crossed arms resting on his knees, and glared at Reid.

"Am I to assume *you* are threatening *me*?" Reid straightened, thoughts of his gun spinning.

"I'm only a manager. I can't go against bank operating protocol nor our board." Cavanaugh sat back in the chair.

Reid motioned toward the shot glass. "Like I said, that's good sipping stuff." In a fluid movement, he stood, put his hands in his pockets, and glared. White shrapnel scars puckered along his left arm. "I'll need to talk with Angela and get back to you."

The manager stood, extended his hand, reconsidered the gesture, and lowered it to his side.

Reid turned away.

Cavanaugh stomped back to his office, snarled at his secretary to call the head of the county roads department, and "put him through as soon as possible."

When the phone rang, Cavanaugh answered and rose to close his door against unwelcomed ears.

Out on the sidewalk, Reid thumped out a cigarette and lit up. A pinch of tension crept up his neck and an incessant pulsing began in his temples. The whop-whop-whop of choppers reverberated. Almost three o'clock and the heat layered down on him. Sweat pimpled across his upper lip.

He climbed into the pickup and drove toward the Blue Star. An afternoon beer would pave the way through his evening chores.

Chapter 33
Tobacco Work

April 1970

Joe stopped by the Holcombe Farm on his way home from the feed store. He stayed in the truck and tapped the obligatory short beeps. Bugle trotted out, bayed in deep bass notes announcing Joe's arrival.

Poking his head out of the curing barn, Reid stopped work and strode toward the pickup. Face blank, he did not wave or signal hello.

Joe stepped down from the cab, leaned against the metal truck bed, and rested his forearms on the side, hands dangling open. He frowned, his vulnerability at the feed store looping. Still, there was more than one way to manipulate power.

"What brings you out?" Reid indifferently propped on the opposite side of the truck, took his cap off, and scratched through his sweaty hair. Beads of dirt lined his elbow creases and caked under his fingernails. He gestured to the stacked bags with his cap. "Looks like you've been by the feed store."

"Yeah. Pappy needed more hog pellets."

"That sow farrow?" asked Reid.

"Had ten. They all fat and healthy. Even that one got the hind tit doing good." Joe half-smiled, then lapsed silent into an unreadable face.

Reid dangled the cap between his hands shifted his feet, and frowned, uncomfortable with small talk.

Finally, Joe spoke. "Troublesome thing now is that Pappy got to pay cash for everything. Know anything 'bout that?"

"Oh? I thought Angela set a tab up for y'all. What happened?" He replaced the cap.

"Old man Shipman changed his mind. No credit."

Reid cocked his head to the side. "He say why?"

"Whitey don't need a reason when it comes to us." Joe straightened. He gripped the side of the truck.

The two men bristled, their bodies taut.

****

In Vietnam, segregation had vibrated as strong as it did in the South. The white-black taboos held for southern grunts while in camp, only dissolving in the field. Color faded to gray when on patrol or under fire. Each soldier protected every back without thought to anything but staying alive, remaining whole.

Joe had been wounded, almost killed, heeding that unwritten code. He'd undergone surgery and rehab for months in Landstuhl, Germany, and then transferred to Maryland's Walter Reid Medical Center for additional rehab. A full six months of letters were sent before Joe would board a transport home to South Carolina. When he finally stepped off the plane at Frogmore Airport and into his mamma's embrace, he had dropped his cane and held her with all his pain and triumph and love.

****

Reid stood quiet and then said in a steady voice, "You're probably right about that. They're also after y'all to get to us, force us to sell."

"Is that how you figure it?"

"Yeah. I know those folks and the meanness they can stoop to. If I can't get anyone to work, I lose everything. Right now, I'm needing the plants topped. Still have picking and curing and putting by in front of us too."

"Maybe folks leery of getting mixed into cracker trouble. Maybe they remember old Holcombe and his stingy ways."

"I'll admit that old man could get a bit gruff and tight with money," Reid said. "Angela's different. She laid the law out to me. Said she and Jim Guy worked too hard trying to understand and get changes started. Said the entire South's got to think different."

"Yeah. Change." Joe spoke slow, watched Reid's face for a signal. "That mean you too? Think you gonna change?"

"I think I'm doing fine like I am. But Angela doesn't agree. She says I'm like everyone in the South. Racist. Says we have to change. Learn to do what's right."

"You mean, like let us vote? Go to school wherever? Kinda be like regular white people?"

"Damn you. Don't push things." Reid jerked his cap off and whacked it against the truck side. "Gotta take things slow. People don't like change."

"Ah, huh. I thought as much," Joe said. He gazed off into the fields. "I saw a peasant woman one time in a rice field. She was kneeling and crying and holding them crushed little seedlings in her hands like they was babies." He shook his head and stared directly at Reid.

"I don't like watching Pappy worrying over his hogs and his vegetables. Having to tolerate being called 'boy' when he's got gray hair. Don't like the word uncle when it gets used like a pet dog name. Him having to step off the sidewalk when anyone white goes by. Likely to get hit if he so much as accidently brushes against a person. Don't like Mamma being looked through, worked early and late, and never able to say what's on her mind."

Reid did not respond immediately, simply gazed down and shifted. He pushed back from the truck bed, fists clenched at his side.

Joe straightened, his eyes narrowed and voice rough. "I ain't up to being treated like no stray cat neither. We carry our fair share, pay our own way."

Insects seemed to pause in their buzzing and the birds with their calls. Although not quite full summer, the heat cooked down, drying the landscape. A car rattled by on the county road, followed by a rooster tail of dust. Bugle scratched at her stomach and huffed.

Reid, still rigid, nodded, leaned against the truck again.

Joe stood silent, resumed a blank face, and then spoke low, "If that summer offer for work still open, I'll take it."

Reid glanced up quickly, leaned over, and wiped a hand down his pants, leaving smeared dirt. "I can use the help. Tobacco's more work than I remembered."

"That so? Hard to exactly remember how much work tobacco really is, ain't it?" Joe shifted, snorted, and allowed his face to soften.

"What about stepping into cracker trouble?"

"Not interested in trouble no matter the color. I had my share in Nam. Right now, I need work," Joe said. "I plan on leaving here come September and I want to be sure Mamma and Pappy got extra before I go. Besides,

I'll need some traveling money. That means work." Joe crossed his arms. "I'll have to be paid cash ever week."

"Not sure I can swing it every week. I was thinking more every month. With a check. Keeps me on track and helps Angela when she does taxes."

"You know people like us don't have no bank. Can't use no check. Need cash money." Joe stared off down the drive, the crush of prejudice weighed on him. He realized once again, the war and his service changed nothing. Life in South Carolina stayed the same. He cleared his throat and said, "We might be able to do every other week. Got to be cash though. You swing that?"

Reid wiped his forehead, took his cap off, thumped it against his leg, glanced up, and said, "Okay I'll figure a way, so no one pays attention. In the meantime, we'll need you every day, full day. We've got to finish topping, gather a crew, and run the picking. After the first barn's cured, we'll have to get started on unstringing and packing for auction."

"You talk like I never worked no tobacco. I was in the fields learning while you play basketball with the other white boys. I stay in them fields while you off to big time Clemson." Joe stood straight, shoved his hands in his pockets, and frowned. He did not offer any further comment.

Reid allowed his gaze to drift across the supplies in the pickup. He scuffed his foot in the sand, took a deep breath, and backed up a step before he said, "Okay. I need us to understand each other."

"Not my first-time dancing this here honky-tonk tune. I know what to do. Work this summer only. Neither me nor Pappy field hands," Joe said, his face blank, a skill he had cultivated from his youth and perfected in the military.

"That seems fair. I hope to have the farm settled by the end of the season."

"Cash only? Every two weeks?"

"Cash only. Two weeks."

Joe, face still blank, replied, his tone curt. "Long as you stay fair and reasonable, I do any sweat job you want. My people working tobacco from the time they babies hanging on they mamma's tit."

He opened the truck door and swung into the old vehicle, rested his elbow out the open window. "I know tobacco."

Neither man offered to shake hands.

****

It was after dark, almost nine, by the time Joe unloaded the feed and stacked it in the barn. A heavy molasses odor wafted out the open door. He thought of rice cakes wrapped in banana leaves, gooey clumps he had bought from Saigon street vendors whenever the opportunity arose. Despite the pleasant memories, Joe kept muttering about that snarled country, comparing it to the South as if a painted whore, faithless and mercenary. He loved her heat, her cattail-lined rivers, and afternoons spent fishing with a cane pole. He deeply resented walking on ground glass every time he dealt with a white man. No matter the country.

Pretty Sal followed him as he closed the corn crib and checked the roosting chickens before walking toward the house.

A bare lightbulb hung over the sink. A second bulb, on an electric umbilical cord over the kitchen table, cast a yellow glow across the room. Calvin sat at the table worn smooth by generations of Terrell, his hands around a glass of buttermilk. Mary bustled around reheating supper.

Joe opened the screen, causing it to creak and complain. He wiped his feet. "I see you ain't fixed that old door yet. A dab of oil would keep it from screeching. Sound sets my nerves on edge."

"Got no need to keep that door quiet. It happen to be my alarm system."

"What kind of system is that?"

"Someone try to sneak in, I hear 'em. Clout them on they head." Calvin cackled despite anxiety lines around his eyes, and then grew serious. "You're late. Already dark out there."

"Sure enuf."

"Everything okay?"

"Yeah, Pappy."

"You tell me straight. Don't need no lip. What took so long?"

Chapter 34
Feedstore Incident

May 1970

Joe glanced at his father and closed the door. "That skinflint Shipman not at the store. Only his hired trash there. Right away, that cracker says he couldn't let me have no feed. Says Shipman left orders not to sell to likes of us."

"Damn," Calvin said.

Joe snorted and continued. "Don't matter. Once that redneck sees I got cash, he swivels around, look to see if anybody else in the store watching. I put the money on the counter and step back. He reaches out, careful not to touch me, and pick it up. He tell me be quick, load everything my own self. Say it's already closing time. He make like he busy trying to close up while he stuff that money in his own pocket." Joe rolled his sleeves above his elbows, picked up a kitchen towel, and slung it over his shoulder.

"Damn," Calvin said. "Long as that feller don't call the sheriff or old Shipman don't find out, we're okay. We know we need to get our feed late when Mr. Sticky-fingers is working."

Joe lathered his hands and continued talking. "Well, I see things in this racist town not changed a'tall since I left. Place and folks here like always, so I stopped off at Holcombe's place. Had to check out a few things."

"Holcombe? Why you do a thing like that? 'Specially since y'all bristling at each other."

"Needed to see if that redneck serious about work. At first, it don't seem smart to me hunkering in too close to them people. Didn't want nothing to do with them. Now I'm thinking we might need them. At least for a time."

"Need them? How you figure?" Calvin cupped his hands around the sweating glass of buttermilk.

"You go tell Miss Angela you try her offer one year on salary. Tell her, that work out okay, then you take on another year." He rinsed his hands, flicked water off his fingers, began to dry, and continued speaking. "You look after you own self and Mamma first. Don't take no guff off them white people."

"What you gonna do?"

"That Holcombe boy coming round." Joe half-smirked and continued to dry his hands on a dish towel, all the while speaking in a steady voice. "He's beginning to see changes got to happen. He needing us too. He finally says he'd pay me cash. I tell him I'm going on to Howard come fall, not working no longer, even for folding stuff. Me and him come to an understanding." Joe hung the cloth on a nail and sat down at the table.

"I still gonna be going to the church Sundays and prayer meeting nights." Mary glared at both men. "I keep up with our people that way too. They all got information and news to say. White people always talking around and over us. They don't realize we hear them even if they looking right through us. We knows them better than they knows themselves. Besides, I can call on the Lord while I'm getting the local news." She lifted her chin, humpf'd at the men, and set a pot of turnip greens on the table. She stuck a serving spoon in and wiped her hands on her apron.

"You go to that old church, see what's going on," Joe said, "but you use the backroads. Circle round when you need to. Right now, a lot of folks on edge." He punctuated his remarks with a fork jab into a ham slice.

"This place still gives me the willies with trash driving around with they truck gun racks full," Calvin said. "Ever notice how they always be chewing on a tobacco plug? Nasty habit."

"Coupla years back, things got in an uproar," Mary said, "with activists drifting through and that Dr. King talking against the draft. He be in jail but still talking, guiding us. Poking at the white man. You gone in the Marines then." Mary leaned across the table and handed Calvin a plate of biscuits and red-eye gravy.

He took the dish and studied Joe. "Times are changing, and some folks say we need to play it harder. Others say don't do nothing to cause them bigots to get worked up and anxious. Lots here still fighting the Civil War, waving Confederate flags, and singing Dixie. Lord knows we don't need no nightriders coming neither." He took a heaping spoon of greens and daubed on hot pepper-sauce.

Goosebumps prickled up Joe's arm. Bus boycotts, marches, sit-ins, and shootings hovered too close in his memory. His sisters and a brother had been part of the black migration from the south to the north years prior. A cousin had been killed by the police during a store holdup when he went in to buy milk. A local judge had ruled the shooting a regrettable misjudgment. Said the police didn't mean to kill his cousin, only meant to get the hold-up man—another black feller. Later, word on the street and around town credited the police with a twofer that day. Joe lived only a few heartbeats away from violence, despite being home again.

"We not done no wrong," Mary said. "We trying to live. We got our rights too. For now, we stay low as we can. I got standing at the bakery, everybody know me, and that helps when I come and go. Southern ladies don't want to do their own baking, so they tell they husbands leave me alone. I mostly worried on you, son. White men real timid of strong young black men. Men like you. They anxious to send you over to them jungles, thinking to use you instead of their own boys to fight that war. Now they scared maybe you done learned too much guns and killing."

Joe stared at his mamma, put his fork down, and nodded. "I know what they thinking. I know. Point is, we done learned stuff. Can't be undone now."

"I sleep more easy when you leave here. Go North."

"North got it own problems," Calvin said.

"Things'll get better when I get up there," Joe said. "People not as prejudiced."

Mary glanced at Calvin and Joe. She spoke in a firm voice. "White people think cause they live close to one of us, or work with us, they not prejudiced. Well, I'm here telling you, I never seen a white person yet, that don't think different when it comes to color of you skin. Don't make no never mind where they come from—North or South." Frowning, she pulled a pan from the oven. "You men start eating before food gets cold." She placed a stone crock on the table and wiped her hands on a dishtowel. "Churned this here butter this morning."

Unspoken doubts still rattled in the air.

Chapter 35
Midnight

June 1970

Heart pounding, mouth dry, and sleepless, Reid sat alone, smoked, and waited.

At midnight, the charcoal-edged voice coughed, a gagging sound, and then words flowed as from a molding soul.

Too many ghosts. They stare. They're always here, floating around me, looking with those dead eyes.

"They were peasants. Collateral damage. Expendable."

I didn't think it would end like this. Did we win?

"Hang in. You're home. Safe."

Got no tribe anymore. Everyone gone. What happened?

"I don't know," Reid said. "Most of the good ones gone. Even those crazy Greenies."

Brass tells you go home, be good boys. They said we were invincible. I need my Spanish-magic lady, my woman. We float up in blue smoke together.

"Yeah, man, I know."

Another cough. *People can't hear. Don't want to know. They need everything clean. Safe. Righteous. We're the good guys. Aren't we?*

"Stay with me. Don't quit. We can do this," Reid

said.

I can't. No one wants a cripple. No room for a whiner.

"No man. Don't say that. We've got to help each other." Reid leaned against the wall, listened to the ragged breathing. "Stay with me. Don't quit. You're safe." He continued in a sing-song chant, tell me okay, tell me okay...tell me..."

Figures, pale as dying neon, flickered against the wall. Reid sweated and stared at them. Finally, the word 'okay' and the figures began a slow fade.

He slipped on his pants and shirt, made coffee, and sat at the kitchen table, arms resting on the surface. When the first tatters of day appeared, he stood, sat his cup on the drain rack, and went outside. He stared at the farm.

The asphalt and tar-shingled curing barn loomed tall on the outer edge of the pasture, near the feedlot. The propane tank for the barn heaters, used for drying, hunkered a few yards away. The familiarity of the land, the morning coolness, the quiet before cockcrow, and mist hovering across the ground—like Nam. His thoughts straddled currents, moved back and forth, swept fate into a dustpan.

At first, he told himself, it's only a job. The adrenaline highs followed by his stomach lurching crash into remorse, regret, and confusion. The cold realization it was more than a job. He walked toward the barn. Bugle trotted beside him. They left a bright green trail in the dew.

A wave of oven-heat hit him when he opened the barn door. The burners were operating effectively, drying the tobacco into doe-soft leaves of burnished bronze, smelling of mellow cigars and shredded smoking-tobacco, a pleasant brown odor.

Only a few more things needed to be put in place.

Chapter 36
Le Thi Linh

February 1968

Often Linh sat outside the Quonset hut next to a spindly tree, somehow miraculously growing on the edge of the compound. Gusting wind blew trash along the gutter. A man scurried down the road and evaporated into the haze.

After Têt, Reid had given her instructions on how to leave the country. Several nights previously, she squatted on her haunches peasant fashion with her brother and talked in whispers, planning their disappearance. Although an extra burden, her brother had several orphaned children he said he could not leave. She packed medicines with additional rice as bargaining chips for them.

Viet Cong infiltrators frightened her the most. They killed indiscriminately out of party loyalty—and fear. She had volunteered to serve, and now, could not abandon her country. Nor leave the Communist Party.

She worried the fighters too wounded to travel, would become prisoners or be shot. She struggled with concerns over older peasants, crippled, their rice fields and homes destroyed. She agonized over the children, without care or parents. Her war contributions, offered on a knife's edge, required information be collected, munitions hidden for later, medical care dispensed, and, sometimes, the sabotage of American equipment.

Most of all, filial obligations to her dead husband and her ancestral duties to her parents could not be ignored. Reputation and piety lived beyond the grave.

Part of an unrecognized hairnet of obstructions, she melted into the chaos. She could not leave. Vietnam was her home.

Chapter 37
Working Tobacco

June 1970

Carolina heat beat down on Reid and Joe. By ten, the sun swallowed the boney morning cool as they worked down the tobacco rows topping the plants and pinching suckers. The flowering stalks, shoulder level, swayed while they worked. Between the plant movement and green nicotine, the men grew nauseous. Not generally inclined to talk, they nonetheless fell into a companionable banter to keep their minds occupied.

"We got goddamn gnats and flies here, but those Nam leeches were nasty suckers," Reid said.

"Naw man, the mosquitos were the worst. Those sumabitches moved in hordes. Got in your ears and mouth. Kept you from talking," Joe chuckled. "Sometimes you couldn't even see for them things."

"Heat'd get to you there even faster than here. Coupla times I thought I'd hurl riding those choppers. They'd be overloaded trying to take off from a hot zone, blood stink all over the inside. Bucking. Swaying. Me sweating under all that gear."

"Man, you scared you get your pecker shot off. That makes anybody sick." Joe cackled and slapped his leg.

"And you tell me you weren't scared?"

"You just don't get it. None y'all white boys never did." Joe held his arms wide and shook his head. "You were messed up in you head before that draft notice ever come in the mail. You, your balls, your head. Everything messed up."

"How you figure?"

"Y'all bought that destroy Communism line. Bought the godless governments taking over the world talk. Course, we got LBJ and he's not exactly what I'd call a save-our-souls-preacher."

Joe snorted and continued to talk. "Y'all graduate, think you save the world, get excited with those uniforms, free guns, and sign up for Vietnam. Y'all don't even let ink dry on them diplomas. You crazy. Us bros got enough sense to wait. They want us, they gotta come fetch us."

"You'd think different if Communists land on your doorstep," Reid said.

"Bomb, bomb, bomb—it's all you understood. Y'all think you playing dominos or something."

"Come on, man. Uncle Sugar's got our best interest at heart." Reid smiled.

"Humph. Maybe your interest but not mine. Two wars going on in Nam, one with Viet Cong and one between y'all and us. Them Cong should have sat back and waited to see who won. Saved a bunch of misery." Joe stopped topping and studied Reid. "Come to think of it, government only got government interest to look out for. Politicians trying to keep their job on your back. You think about that. Their job. Your back."

"Sweet hell. You had as much to lose as me."

"You crazy as a rooster locked out of the hen house." Joe glared at Reid, his voice rough. "We bros already know we get rousted by a town cop anytime his old lady didn't put out the night before. Whitey got a hangover, he think busting a nappy head the cure."

"Come on, man. Not like that at all." Reid paused, stared at Joe, and flicked a tobacco top down the row. "You need to work harder. Stay with it."

"What you say. You try walking up them courthouse steps in a black skin and see if you can even *register* to vote. Try driving a car at night through town."

Reid bent down, hands on his knees, and spat. "Hot as that hellhole was, it felt cold when the monsoons arrived, especially around Nha Trang. Always surprised me," He stood, wiped his face, and continued down the row topping plants.

Joe shook his head, glanced at Reid, and silently cut the blossoms off several more stalks. "Ever thing a surprise to you."

"I remember the rain coming down in sheets," Reid said. "Constant pounding. Messed with my head."

"I don't need that stuff. Nobody does. Them people love that country, I say let'em keep it."

"You sound like one of those doves. That it?" Reid's face scrunched into a cross between a frown and a smile.

"Who you call coward?" Joe scowled at Reid. "I served with distinction and honor—got the papers to prove it. Now I'm home, I don't need no white boy strutting round, acting he's better than me."

****

The military, fully integrated on paper, did not in practice honor racial equality. Raw was the only way Joe could describe his experience around that omission.

He had spent time in Saigon bamboo-bars and done male posturing whenever knock-off whiskey flowed too fast. Sometimes a simple raised fist, made famous during the '68 Olympics, triggered a brawl. Word on the street was only blacks, Hispanics, and poor white Southerners got drafted. Bantering with Reid brought those incidents back in sharp detail. More than once, Joe had welcomed guard duty in a downpour to clear his head after a long night.

Carolina heat waves shimmered watery across tobacco plants as endless as the sea. The sun boiled toward meridian.

****

The two men fell silent, lost in separate thoughts, and threaded their way down the rows, plant by plant. Sweat coated the hair on Reid's forearms, matted Joe's wiry fuzz. Tar stuck to their hands and dirt beads settled in elbow creases.

Joe smiled, topped another plant, and tossed pink blossoms over his shoulder. "You might toss working this here tobacco, but least you ain't gonna get blowed into the next world."

"The next world? You think it's better than this one?"

"Maybe for you honkeys. Not for us dudes."

"Aw, Joe, my man. You're talking cynical in your old age."

"I ain't old." Joe snorted, thumped his chest, and topped another plant. "I'm realistic."

"You call going to college realistic?" Reid said. "I've got a degree—signed and stamped with that little gold seal—and here I am, ready to puke, working a gall-dern tobacco patch. Which, I might add, the bank is stealing out from under me with a foreclosure. Damn bloodsuckers. Crooked suits."

"All a matter of perspective, my man, a matter of perspective. Don't mean nothin."

"This work doesn't even have the jack-up of one afternoon patrol," Reid said. "I miss the highs, the rush."

"You peckerwoods get off on some seriously dumb mess. I ain't wanting to die over no high from no war. Now, a woman, that's different. That's my kind of adrenaline rush." Joe bent over laughing.

Reid grinned, wiped his face, snapped off a sucker, and tossed it on the ground. As unpleasant as it was, the physicality of the fields and dripping sweat created an odd gratification.

Again, they grew silent, preoccupied in thought as they worked down the rows, accompanied by the swish of nicotine-laden leaves. At the end of every four-row loop, they stopped for water, sat in the shade of the plants, and scrubbed sand on their hands to loosen the tar.

Joe reached for water bucket, face expressionless, drank from a stainless-steel dipper, and passed it to Reid, flaunting the southern taboo of shared drinking cups. Reid paused. He shrugged, filled the dipper, and drank.

Separate and unequal, the two men had followed the same, yellow-painted footprints into the entry portal at Marine Corps Recruit Depot Parris Island. While they had not served together, they had survived boot and become Marines using the same template.

Grudgingly, Reid stared at Joe, realized the man had moxie. He had slogged through basic training, been wounded, and honorably discharged. He worked hard no matter the endeavor and had plans for himself.

With their discharge, time and events moved past the mud and lost days, not far, only a short step. The Carolina sun dropped a sauna blanket over the field. Insect sounds quieted. Lost in thought and memories, each sweated through the afternoon.

The holiness of war and a hero's welcome home stank like rotten eggs.

Chapter 38
Mary Terrell

June 1970

Mary jerked awake. The lamp was still on and her Bible lay open on her lap. The clock read 12:34 a.m. She listened to the night—the refrigerator humming, the bed creaking as Calvin shifted in his sleep, and somewhere in the house, a cricket fiddled.

Joe had not come in.

She rose from the rocker and peered out the window. Pretty Sal was asleep on the porch. No sign of anyone. The silence and Joe's absence troubled her.

****

Days before, two farm boys had deliberately bumped into Mary and Calvin as they left Winn-Dixie on their way home with groceries.

They knocked Calvin against the outside door and then darted away. He stumbled, and, to avoid falling, grabbed at Mary's arm, dropping their sacks. A bag of sugar busted on the sidewalk, the crystals sparkling in the sun. A flour sack landed with a soft plop, the bag split. A breeze whirled it away in white flurries. Eggs, carefully balanced on top, lay cracked and slimy at their feet. Several apples rolled across the parking lot.

Returning a grocery cart to the store, a pimply-faced bag boy stopped and helped them pick up what scattered items could be salvaged. He murmured something unintelligible, glanced around to see who might be watching, and offered the cart. Confused, he did not suggest replacing any ruined item, but only held his head low as he scurried back into the store.

****

Mary woke Calvin. "Son's not home. Something's happened. What should we do?"

Calvin, sleep heavy, staggered out of bed, pulled on his overalls, and slipped his feet into boots without stopping for socks.

"You stay here in case he come home. Anyone you don't know come up, leave out the back and hide. I'll walk through the woods to the blacktop; see I can spot anything going on." Calvin frowned, rubbed his hand across his face, and gave Mary's arm a squeeze. "Joe is a good boy. He'll be okay."

She frowned and cut the light. Calvin slipped outside. Pretty Sal rose and stood next to him, her hackles up, whining deep in her throat. Mary stared off into the dark and shifted uneasily. Calvin patted her arm, stepped off the porch, and disappeared down the dirt road.

****

Joe stopped three times to wipe blood out of his eyes. With his hand out the truck window, he popped his fingers, flecking droplets off into the dark. He drove. Nausea rose in his throat and a heaviness crept into his limbs.

"Keep driving. You can do this," he said aloud. "Take the dirt roads home, drive through them back woods. Stay off the paved roads. You can do this." He spoke soft, his voice encouraging him. "Any whites out looking, they keep to the county hardtops. Besides, they know I fight. They not anxious to catch up with me a second time."

At the turn to the Terrell property, he cut the engine, slipped the old truck out of gear, coasted down the road, and into the back yard. "No sense alerting anyone. Better to slip in real quiet," he said to himself. "Thank you, Uncle Sugar, for the training."

His silent appearance at the window startled Mary. As soon as she saw his face, she realized there had been a fight, and began to mutter under her breath.

"You come in. I get you fixed. Good thing I had lots of brothers in my family and know how to handle this." She pulled the kitchen shades before turning on the light.

She dabbed methiolate on a cut above Joe's eye and swabbed his knuckles, then fashioned an ice pack from an old towel, and pressed it against a swelling on his forehead. She threaded a sewing needle. Joe held the towel in place and braced himself. She worked quick and gentle, stitched the cut closed, dabbed it again with medicine, and fashioned a fresh ice pack for him.

Afterwards, Mary clomped around the kitchen, expounded on various bits of gossip, replaced the medicine bottle cap, and stood before Joe, hands on her hips.

"You tell me again what happened. What caused you to get beat up?"

"I told you, Mamma," Joe said. "White trash jumped me outside that movie house. Three of them lay for me. Damn cowards. Came up, started cussing, went to hitting before I said a word."

"Watch the mouth. That's you mamma you be speaking to." Calvin, from the woods, had seen Joe glide by in the pickup and Mary draw the shades. He had slipped in through the back door.

"Yes, sir," Joe said and continued his tale. "They hopping around, hollering and hitting and cussing. Zena got knocked down. I jerk her up and tell her run. I think they broke my rib. Maybe two."

"Who's Zena?" asked Mary.

"My date."

"Why I ain't never heard 'bout this Zena woman?"

"I don't have to keep you up on all my business. I'm a grown man with man needs. Besides, she got away. I don't think she's hurt. Scared, but not hurt." Joe shifted the ice pack. "I check on her later."

"You be careful 'bout dipping into the pudding when you don't know the flavor." Calvin gave Joe a penetrating frown and slipped his boots off. "You keep on pressing you luck and next thing you be kilted like you cousin."

"Those trash had no call to do that cousin like they done. They kill him cause they could. Plain and simple," Mary said. "Ain't no season on our kind. Don't even need a hunting license."

"I know, Mamma. I know."

"God didn't send you home safe to turn around and let peckerwoods lynch you. Especially when you puttin it to some woman," Calvin said.

"I ain't lynched. I ain't putting it to no woman. I've been through worse than this in Nam. I'll take care of what needs doing." Joe glared at his mamma, goose bumps prickling hair along his arms. He flashed a full-face grin, then grew solemn. "Lucky it's dark along that there alley. Them cowards can't see me in the shadows else they get at me worse. For once, black is better."

Despite their concern, Mary and Calvin laughed.

"Black *is* better—least ways at night in an alley fight," Mary said.

"God didn't send me home to go sliding off like some whipped dog," Joe said. "I'm not wanting to be fighting again, but I can't live less than a man. Sooner or later, I reckon we all got to double down on those stump-jumpers. South ain't changed. She' still a whore."

"Watch you mouth. This here where we live. This where we *gots* to live," Calvin said.

****

Headlines from 1964 materialized again in Joe's head: Philadelphia, Mississippi. Black church burned. Three civil rights workers arrested by local police, allegedly speeding. Several hours in jail. Released to the Ku Klux Klan. Found shot to death, murdered, several hours later.

Joe thought this was probably the only time honkeys knowingly buried two whites and a black in the same grave. In a single night, the "other Philadelphia" had gained a forever place in Mississippi history.

Killing had happened in Vietnam, but there, especially in the field, Joe saw it as a "Marines against Viet Cong" scenario. He had a sense of a fair chance there, not helpless execution. Except in the case of the peasant farmers and villagers. He stared straight ahead and thought about things you simply filed away for reference.

"Them crazy crackers kill you for looking at them

wrong." Mary moved around the kitchen with the authority of a field sergeant. She handed Joe four aspirins and a glass of water. "That's all I got."

"Your mamma's right," Calvin said. "You need to be leaving. Between this pushing stuff and that feed store mix up, now this here fight, you need to go before they find a reason to throw you in jail. You *know* what happen next."

"We tight on money. Y'all need to have a little set by before I go, 'specially if we can't work tobacco," Joe said.

"Naw, we okay. We get you traveling money together fast." Calvin's face scrunched into a deep frown. "I see if'n Miss Angela help send word to Miss Ellie, ask we hide you in Beaufort. You lay low until we find a safe way outta here. We contact Mary's people out on the water. Between us all, we send you away early. You leave this town before it's too late."

"We lay low for a spell too," Mary said.

"I ain't let that Mo-rine brother of Miss Angela think I'm coward. I'll stay right here and work the fields until time to leave in September. I do what I tell I'm gonna do."

"You ain't yellow," Calvin said. "We knows you a man and not scared of them tobacco-slobbering, mouth breathers. We know you can handle you self. But I tell you the truth, you can't do no good for nobody if you dead. Civil rights or marches or voting or anything come to nothing if you dead. I'm you daddy and you do what I tell you."

White, the Vietnamese color of mourning, contrasted with white as symbolic purity—even for a pregnant bride. Black symbolized death, grief, and fear.

A color usually worn by widows and grieving families—and Viet Cong guerrillas. Paradoxically, being 'in the black' was considered a good thing. Joe played with the observation, stared at his hands, and pondered on the significance of color.

After a moment, he glared up. "You wrong, Pappy. Wrong. Being a man, walking upright is worth dying for. I fought for this damn country and I deserve better than a beating when I come home." His thoughts sharpened.

Mary examined Joe's face, "You right. You deserve more as a man, especially coming back from hell like you done."

****

Monday, when Joe arrived at the Holcombe farm, Reid's anger at Joe's battered face and bent walk took them both by surprise. Reid had gritted his teeth after hearing of the canceled feed store credit and Winn-Dixie pushing incident.

Joe waved off his questions, joked about loose women on the prowl, and husbands that couldn't hold their liquor. Joked about wobbly older men trying to grocery shop.

But Reid, in his white soul, understood this progression into violence, slow at first, then flaring in one quick jump. He let it drop—at least for the time being.

****

Both whites and blacks patronized parts of Willington: the Winn-Dixie grocery, post office, hardware store, drug store, and auto supply. The movie theater catered to both, but only allowed blacks in the balcony. A barbershop, beauty salon, four churches, and several restaurants remained strictly segregated.

A greasy barbeque shack, home beauty shop, two churches, and school to ninth grade served the Negro community.

Mary, a baker at Noe's Fine Pastries on east Davenport Street, started before daylight. By noon, with shoppers rushing to finish errands on their lunch hour, Noe asked her to work the counter, bag bread and sweets. He worked the cash register.

Town whites gossiped over the counter—the latest wedding, "premature" baby, divorce, city scandal, or church bazaar—never acknowledging Mary's presence. She filed overheard information away for later. Being talked over as if invisible irritated her, but sometimes it proved useful.

Angela, on the other hand, gathered a different tale in scraps and pieces, supplemented by gossip. By Wednesday, information Angela garnered and Mary's eavesdropped discussions, offered a complete picture.

The summer stretched out hot and dangerous.

Chapter 39
Midnight

July 1970

The disembodied charcoal voice climbed an octave. Fingernails on a chalkboard, the voice scratched against Reid's hearing.

Didn't mean to keep sucking on those brown water bottles. Couldn't help curling up in smoke. Just wanted something between me and the world. Needed something between me and the churchwomen. Something other than the good citizens.

"I know, man," Reid said. "Something between."

Gotta put the fires out. Everything's burning. I still smell that stink.

"Hold on. Things will get better. You have a life here. You're home. Tell me okay."

Too many dead. Too much time. We never should have been there. It was their country.

Reid pulled his bed sheets into a wad, realized his hands were sweating. "No. You're wrong. They needed help. They were fighting, pushing the Communist out. We had to help them."

Do you remember our beach?

"I remember."

We never helped. We destroyed.

"We were the good guys."

We killed everything that moved. Sometimes things that didn't move.

"We did what we thought we were sent to do," Reid said.

Why did they kill the babies?

"They killed their own. They raped their own." Reid wrung his hands, washing them over and over.

A country of water. A place of sweat.

"Yes, water. Monsoons. Rice paddies. Rivers. The sea."

Water ties us—you and me. Those people tied by water too. I should have stayed.

The voice coiled behind Reid's eyes and plunged splinters into his chest.

"Don't quit. You served with honor. You're safe. Say okay."

Reid rolled to the edge of the bed and lit a cigarette. He reached under his pillow, groped for the revolver, fondled the coldness, and stroked the blue gray of it. He placed it on his nightstand.

The cigarette burned down. He lit another off the glowing butt, struggled against exhaustion. Listened. Not until the repeated okay did Reid slide the pistol under his pillow again, dress and step onto the back porch barefooted. He sat on the stoop. Daylight hovered hours away.

He'd left her. So what?

Chapter 40
Le Thi Linh

Late April 1967

Several klicks outside his base camp, Reid had passed a makeshift Vietnamese civilian clinic compound. A Quonset hut sat among a jumble of small sheds and storage areas, covered with tattered pieces of plastic and corrugated metal. A freestanding tent, open sides yet suffocatingly hot, offered shade for the weekly medicine and food distribution. Scattered crude shelters housed the families of wounded and sick, until they either died, or found a way back to their village. Outside cooking rings, in various stages of use, smoked constantly, like trash burn-barrels dotting Reid's rural Carolina homescape.

The clinic grounds, hard-packed in the dry season and a mini-swamp during monsoon, belched with the stench of vomit, feces, and rotting food. Mothers with children and old men waited, squatted peasant fashion on their haunches.

Monday, returning from an errand, Reid heard angry voices and a shot as he approached the clinic compound. He jogged forward. The back of a Marine led ARVM platoon disappeared down the track.

A Vietnamese crone lifted screaming children from a wooden cart pulled by a water buffalo. The animal groaned. Blood dripped from its thick neck. A slender woman hurried out to help. He stared at the two women and children.

"Goddamn it all to hell. Them sonsabitches didn't need to shoot the buffalo." He slung his rifle over his shoulder and, still muttering, started toward the women and children.

The crone launched a verbal torrent at Reid. She bustled into the Quonset hut with two toddlers clinging to her pants, a squalling baby in her arms, and a young girl struggling to keep pace.

The slender, younger woman took a small child in her arms, wiped his tears, and leaned down to stroke the head of a somewhat older boy standing stoic beside her, sucking his thumb. A white scar ran through her eyebrow and a thick rope of hair swung down her back.

Reid moved toward the cart, intent on the children. "I'll help."

She held her hand up, palm out. "You have done enough. Take your killing and go away." Her face, distorted in anger, halted him.

"You Americans are not part of our country. You are savages. Leave." She turned toward the Quonset hut and carried the child inside, its grubby hand still clutching her braid. A diminutive girl, mucus and tears covering her face, grasped the hem of the woman's top and trotted screaming beside her. The older boy followed. They dissolved into the darkness.

The woman pricked Reid's conscience long after he left.

Chapter 41
Reid Holcombe

May 1967

Two weeks elapsed before Reid had time to stop by the makeshift clinic, find the woman, and offer payment for the buffalo.

She shook her head. "Too late. *Ils sont partis.* They have gone. Auntie, oldest boys, and the girl walk north. Villagers take small ones."

"Then use this money for the other children."

She stuffed the proffered money into her pocket and strode away.

Reid called after her. "I can help with supplies. What's your name?" He pulled his helmet off and trailed her into a fetid smelling hut.

"This is my clinic." She waved her arm across the rows of cots.

Some people sat, legs dangling off their beds. Others moaned feebly. A toddler watched him with impenetrable eyes, holding onto a cot frame as if tethered. Flies buzzed and dabbed around anything moist. Scraps of mosquito netting floated exhausted in an occasional breeze.

"Can I pay for the buffalo?"

She regarded him a long minute before she spoke, her voice firm. "The boys will make fine NVA regulars.

You helped them choose."

"What's your name?"

"Show me the color of your heart and maybe I will tell you my name."

"You Viet Cong?" he asked.

"Would you believe me?"

"No." The words loomed cold in Reid's mouth. "Well, maybe." He watched her move among the cots, her hair shining iridescent blue whenever she stepped into the sunlight. Her clothes covered her body yet outlined its details. Sexy and modest in a single stroke. She moved with a grace he had never noticed before.

"You may or may not be Charlie, but you're a damn fine-looking woman."

She did not respond, simply disappeared in the half-light of the ward.

He shrugged, unsure if she didn't hear or simply ignored him.

Chapter 42
Young Joe Terrell

June 1966

Calvin turned the radio on as Mary dished up breakfast. Joe scraped a chair out from the table and plopped down. They had barely settled down when James Meredith's admission to the University of Mississippi was announced.

"Ole Miss all white. That man finally done got in. If he can do it, then I can too." Joe sat bold upright, his fork halfway to his mouth, and eyes wide. Mary's face went blank before it curled into a half-smile then shifted into an angry frown. She leaned toward Joe. "You watch yourself, Mr. Big Britches. That man a long way from you. Eat your breakfast." She pursed her lips into a scowl.

"President Kennedy sent troops down to help," Joe said. He leaned forward, spilled scrambled eggs off his fork, spoke rapidly, and looked from Mary's face to Calvin's and back. "I'm going to college in two years. Why not go to a white college?"

"People gonna get killed they get to thinking beyond they selves," Mary said. "We need to wait. See how things turn out."

Joe plunked his fork down. "But Mama, you know things got to change. Even the President doing his part.

He sent help."

Mary pointed her finger at Joe and clucked through her teeth. "President mighta sent troops to Mississippi. I ain't sure he's gonna do that for nobody here in South Carolina. Done told you, eat them eggs."

"Son let's wait a while and see what happens," Calvin said. "Them white people always looking out for each other before they looking for us. This here ain't done yet." Calvin rose from the table, scuffed across the kitchen, and put on his weather-beaten hat.

"Where you gwain?" Mary wiped her hands on her apron and stared at Calvin. "You didn't finish eating. Why I worry with cooking, you not gonna eat?"

Silent, his face furrowed and lips tight, Calvin shook his head, pushed the screen door open, and went outside.

Mary, still for a moment, scowled, and then pointed her finger at Joe. "In the meantime, Mr. Big, you get your skinny butt out yonder and hep your pappy."

"I ain't finished breakfast." Joe picked his fork up.

"You pappy down in his back. Gwain now and hep him with chores. You eat later." She snorted and flicked him away with her hand.

No sense arguing. Mary's word was household law. He grabbed a biscuit and slouched out chewing.

Getting off the farm and away from tobacco became Joe's looming objective. He wanted college, wanted more than his segregated community, wanted to see the world, and wanted choices.

Then Freedom Summer 1964 dawned with bus riders and voter registration drives. Activists on their way south, sought out safe stopovers and local information on what threatened ahead. The Terrell family began to breath in the changes.

In the Willington community, Mary offered food and pallets on her floor to young blacks and whites traveling the "Rights Road." She swept the church after they finished meetings, fixed sandwiches, and sometimes offered supper.

Joe took note of workers' exuberance and verve as they ate his mamma's collards and cornbread, him alongside, listening. Activists argued over the best methods for challenging authority, how to handle an arrest, and their dreams for a better day. They spoke of life in Boston, Chicago, Buffalo, and places "up North."

Joe's adolescent imagination vibrated at young men and women with their lunch counter sit-ins defying white screams and abuse, sitting nonviolent. Hair on his arms prickled at TV images of Woolworth lunch counters and later Greyhound buses running south.

Mary and Calvin, chilled at the prospect of spilled blood, white or black, sat stoic and silent, faces deeply lined.

Nevertheless, the seed planted in Joe's mind that morning at breakfast, fertilized by a heady flow of strangers, and his parents' quiet activism, sprouted and grew.

"In two years, Mamma, I'll be eighteen. I'll graduate high school and go away—up North probably—to college. I need to get in on this activism stuff. Students all over working and I'm not gonna be left behind." Joe spoke with youthful invincibility.

Mary pressed her lips into a tight, narrow line. "I know how old you are. I know when you graduate. I know more'n you about what's out there."

Calvin threw her a look filled with fear and pride. He sat silent.

Mary bowed up again and continued. "I tell you something else, Mr. Big-know-it-all. Whites like to be told how kind they are, how just, and that God is pleased with them. Don't a day go by at that bakery that I don't be ready to tell some white woman how pretty they little girl is or how I held back yeast rolls especially for her—when I got a whole pan in the rear. Whites don't know us. But we *know* them."

Joe stared at her, mouth open. "But, Mama, I want to see the world. I want to know more than this here racist South Carolina."

Mary leaned back in her chair, arms crossed on her chest. "Stuff'll come."

The black-and-white vortex pulled on him, on Mary and Calvin, and on the black community.

Yet unrecognized, on the periphery of their world, loomed a land of dragons called Vietnam. Humid. Distant. Exotic. Deadly.

Chapter 43
A Burning Cross

July 1970

A whoosh of fire illuminated the dirt road at Calvin and Mary's clapboard house. Smoke billowed from a burning cross and spiraled into the air.

Calvin grabbed Mary, slung a wrap over her house dress, and pushed her toward the back door. Ever practical, she snatched up a frying pan and her shoes, and scuttled out across the porch.

"Run through them woods to Angela's. Ask her come quick." Calvin hollered and shoved Mary outside. "Joe still there working."

She disappeared in the pines brandishing her iron skillet like a club. Brush snagged her dress and briars scratched her. Tiny pinpricks of blood spotted her legs. Heart pounding, she ignored the scratches, hiked her dress above her knees, and ran.

Night sounds paused, the woods silent except for the thrash of the woman, her breath coming in gasps and pants. She ducked under low limbs and around pine trees, running hard.

****

Calvin opened his front door, raised both hands, and shouted. "What y'all want? What y'all want? This here my property."

The fiery cross illuminated three men standing next to a pickup. A heavy-set man held a gas can while a thin fellow in khakis and a medium height, thin nose companion leaned forward grinning, leering at their handiwork.

The fire belched and crackled, licked up into the night.

The razor-nose man leaned forward. "We came by to see you people need eggs. We got a bunch of fresh scrambled ones." The three broke into loud guffaws and slapped each other on the back.

As the cross blazed, Pretty Sal, hackles raised, bayed, and charged the men, teeth snapping before dashing back to the porch, tail tucked. She continued her charge and retreat while Calvin gestured with a sweep of his arms and hollered, "What you want? Get off my property. We got nothing belong to y'all." He stood at the edge of the porch, belly protruding against his overalls, face distorted with fear.

"Where's that hotshot soldier boy of yours? He best not be working for them Holcombe's. He needs to get his ass outta there. No need of his kind roaming around. Not here there ain't. Not now. Not ever."

"He ain't here. He's gone."

"You working for them Holcombe's? I thought we told you people, hang them out to dry. Quit them, leave them struggle on their own."

"Yessah. Miss Angela a widow woman. She need help. Ain't done no wrong." He raised his head defiantly. "Got to have the work. Ain't trying to go against y'all. Just need the work."

"That woman's damn brother home from *Vee-it-nam* can help. Let him do the work. You need to leave them Holcombe's take care their own mess." The bald man pointed at the cross. "This here's your job termination notice."

"Yessah. Yessah." Calvin stood on the edge of the porch. His face gleamed with sweat, hands held up, palms out.

"Next time there'll be more than shoving and smashed eggs at the grocery store. Y'all hear me? Next time we'll burn more'n a cross."

The heavy-set man shifted and stepped back into darkness away from the firelight.

Pretty Sal continued to bay and charge between the house and truck. The razor-nose man swiveled back to the vehicle and jerked a rifle off the gun rack. He aimed at Pretty Sal, pulled the trigger. She yelped and thrashed in a circle.

From the porch, hands waving, Calvin screamed hoarse. "Don't shoot! Don't shoot! Leave my dog alone. Lordy, don't shoot no more." He hobbled off the porch toward Pretty Sal, grimacing with each yelp.

"Damn dog's mad. Got rabies. It's trying to kill me." The shooter bellowed and pumped another bullet into the rifle chamber. "Dog's dangerous."

"No Lordy, she ain't got no rabies. She just scared. She a huntin' dog. Don't shoot no more." Calvin stumbled and sank to his knees beside the dog.

The shooter raised the rifle and sighted.

The heavy-set man shoved the gun barrel down. "Leave the crazy thing alone. She's just a coonhound. We not paid to kill no dog. Git in the truck. We're leaving." He yanked the truck door open and muttering, slid inside.

Angry, the shooter pulled the trigger and glared as

the shot kicked up dirt. He clambered into the truck bed, brandished the rifle, and cussed, words spewing hate as the truck careened down the road.

****

Angela shrieked when Mary bounded on the back porch and burst into the kitchen shouting the house was burning and men trying to kill Calvin. They sprinted out of the house, ran for the tobacco pack shed, and hollered for Reid and Joe.

Joe grabbed Mary by the shoulders and stared at her face. Out of breath from running, she pointed toward the old farm and shook her iron skillet.

"Stay here," he said and dived into his pickup.

Reid grabbed the door frame and vaulted into the seat as Joe accelerated. The truck fishtailed across the ruts toward the Terrell farm.

Mary and Angela, faces creased with worry, followed in Jim Guy's Chevy. The washboard roads jarred their heads as they drove.

By the time they arrived, the trio had gone. The cross still burned, smoke and flames spiraling up.

Reid, Joe, and Angela slung buckets of water on it until the fire hissed and collapsed into embers. Sweating profusely from the heat, Reid doused water on the house clapboard siding as a precaution.

Pretty Sal lay in the yard yowling. Calvin, kneeling over her speckled body, petted and murmured softly. She licked his hand and whimpered. Mary, next to Calvin, stroked the dog's velvet ears and cried, "Lordy, Lordy. They got no call to do this meanness. No call."

Joe knelt next to his parents and examined Pretty Sal. "I seen worse in Nam."

Calvin wiped tears from his face. "She my huntin'

dog. They got no call."

Joe lifted the hound and walked toward his truck.

In the morning light, the blackened pile of two-by-fours still smoldered in the front yard. The house, despite some scorched boards and blistered paint, escaped unscathed. A caustic smell hung in the morning mist.

No one reported the incident to the Colleton County Sheriff.

Chapter 44
Blue Star Grill and Bar

July 1970

Reid had stood by the door a moment and let his eyes adjust to the half-light before he moved into the gin mill. He'd gotten into the habit of dropping by the Blue Star late in the afternoons for a beer.

The bar, mostly empty, had a downcast appearance. Cigarette smoke hovered in gray lines floating across the room. Today, four men playing pool sucked down beers and grew increasingly loud. Heads swiveled toward the door when he entered, and then returned to their pool game.

Reid ordered a Bud and whiskey back. He propped against the bar, knocked back the brown water, and carried his beer to a vinyl stool near the wall. Two older men in work clothes sat at a table talking and nursing beers. A waitress waltzed by, popped her gum, collected empties, and wiped tables.

A dingy sameness to the Blue Star as with all other gin joints, gave Reid a sense of anonymity. He slid his work-cracked hands up and down the sweating beer and took a deep swallow, his Adam's apple bobbing. He ordered a second beer. His tension drained away as the drinks took effect.

"Hey bub, you remember me?" A man wearing

khakis and polo shirt broke away from a group playing pool and swaggered toward Reid, pool cue in hand.

"Yeah, I remember. You're the one studying to be important, that needs numbers. The feller that lets others do their fighting. How could I forget."

"Well, now I got a number for you. Two," Khakis said.

"Two. Meaning what?" Reid said.

"Drop off hiring them two blacks."

"They make you head of farmers' employment services or something?" Reid said.

Khaki twisted toward his buddies and laughed, an unpleasant barking noise. "This here soldier boy got a real sense of humor."

"What business is it of yours who I hire to do my sweat work?"

"I got a vested interest in this county and how things get done around here," Khakis said. "I hear tell you paying them boys regular. That makes it hard on the rest that only pay day labor."

"I wasn't aware you worked, much less had enough gumption to hire someone." Reid's voice rang with a dismissive quality.

The man shifted and stepped closer with his pool cue.

Reid swallowed the last of his beer, rose, and stepped to the bar. He placed his hands flat on the wood.

"Barkeep, one more for me and how 'bout a round for my friends here—my *new* friends." He gestured toward Khakis and the knot playing pool. "No sense letting a *little miscommunication* get in the way of us white folks having a beer together." He smiled and cocked his head.

The bartender drew four brews and set them in a line on the bar. Grinning, Khakis, still basking in his bravado, reached for one and gulped the proffered brew. He licked foam off his lip and sneered at Reid. "This is more like it. No sense getting crosswise with your own kind."

"Give the man another one." Reid smiled and gestured to the others, "Drink up. No harm done. It's all just talk. Don't mean nothing."

Several games of pool later, Khakis handed his cue off to a razor-nose buddy and staggered toward the bathroom, unzipping his fly on the way.

As soon as the john door closed, Reid stood, put money on the bar, and casually walked to the toilets. He opened the door.

A bare light bulb hung in the center of the room between the sink, two urinals, and a single stall. The green-gray walls streaked with water stains, smelled of urine and Pine Sol. Khakis, one hand propped on the wall, glanced up and continued to relieve himself.

The sound of the door banging closed blended seamlessly with a head banging on a porcelain urinal. Khakis stared bewildered at blood dripping from his forehead and broken nose. He rolled from his butt and tried to stand.

Reid grabbed a handful of hair, jerked him to his knees, then squatted down, and whispered in his ear. "That old man and his son work—actually *work regular*—for me. His son and me served in Nam same time. Neither one of them deserve to have you cretins burning crosses in their yard at night. Not only that, but you shot the best damn hunting dog in the tri-counties area. You hear me? The *best hunting dog*. That coonhound didn't die, just crippled up. That makes you lucky. Today." He slammed the man's head against the urinal twice, and continued, "Now, I'd hate for anything further to happen to *my* workers. Or that hound. Understand?" Reid released Khakis' hair, allowed him to slump forward, his mouth hitting the floor. A white tooth lay in a pool of slobber and blood.

Reid straightened his shirt and stepped back into the dimness of the grill.

"Don't mean nothing," he said to no one as he walked outside to his truck.

Chapter 45
Going Bail

July 1970

Ellie considered not answering the office phone. It was after hours and she still had work on the Chamber report to finish.

"Mrs. Holcombe? This is Deputy Kyle Mason, County Sheriff Department."

Ellie fumbled a moment. "Yes, yes, I remember. You called once before. A Clemson buddy of Reid's."

"Yes, Mrs. Holcombe. That's me."

"Please don't tell me another drunken driving thing."

"Well, this time it's a bit more serious. Reid—Mr. Holcombe—got into a confrontation."

Ellie caught her breathe, the gasp audible. "Who? What happened?"

"Well, he got into some kind of dust-up at the Blue Star. Banged a feller up a bit. Sent him to the emergency room. In all fairness, they were both drinking."

"Can you tell me what happened?"

"No, ma'am. I'm stepping outside my bounds just calling. I'll have to ask you to come on down and talk with the duty officer here. Oh, and the bail will be a bit higher than before because the charge is assault."

****

Ellie called Angela and explained the situation in a few curt sentences.

"I'm tapped out," Ellie said. "Nothing left in the saving account and I already have a lien on my station wagon."

"Damn Reid," Angela said. "He's deliberately throwing it all away. Almost like he's trying to get himself killed. I'll meet you at that crossroad gas station and we can drive together." Angela picked up the title to Jim Guy's truck on her way out the door.

****

A blistering heat bore down on the parking lot before arrangements for Reid's release were finalized. Even then, he refused to talk with either of them, another test of wills tainted with violence.

As June ended and July slogged forward, the heat rose, and stress with making bank payments mounted, Reid became more confrontational and unpredictable. He slept restless, disturbed by shapes that eluded him.

He rose before daylight, pulled his clothes on, and stepped out into the morning cool. He closed his eyes, took a deep breath, and opened his eyes to stare at white lotus shimmering in the tall grass. Heard the echo of Buddhist chants and Catholic liturgies. Read Communist slogans and Marine orders written in air. The whoomph of choppers, crinkle of body bags, and slap of Uncle Ho sandals became one sound. Metallic smells blended, hung unpleasant in the air overwhelming the delicate perfume of plumeria. Everything merged.

He sat on the sagging porch steps and sobbed until the physical knot of pain loosened.

Chapter 46
Lunch and Conversation

August 1970

Ellie and Angela met at the Elegant Catfish for lunch the last Wednesday in August. The tobacco season almost behind them, they were anxious to get together and talk.

The Beaufort restaurant touted a home-cooked menu and white tablecloth dining, drew office personnel and groups celebrating everything from birthdays to busines lunches and retirement parties. Twenty-three years in the kitchen, the chef somehow managed to bridge the culinary divide between the blue-collar working man and the white-shirt-and-tie businessman with her truck-stop style of gourmet deep-fried meats, sautéed vegetables, Lowcountry boil, and handmade cheese biscuits.

Old school, Angela ordered the day's special of chicken-fried steak, fresh green beans, and unpeeled mashed potatoes with sweetened iced tea. Ellie chose blackened tuna with coleslaw. They ate slowly, savored the food, and talked work, books, movies and, finally, Reid.

"When did you know?" Ellie said.

"That day Reid came back from the base, after his discharge, he could barely hold himself together. He was a mess. Kept mumbling, he no longer had a tribe, didn't have anyone to take his six."

"His six?" Ellie asked.

"His back. His protection." Angela speared a green bean and continued. "Said he missed his rifle. Felt lost without something for protection. He bought a pistol."

"A pistol?" Ellie pushed slaw around on her plate and nibbled at the fish. No longer hungry, she stared at the food, put her fork down, and took a long swallow of tea.

Conversations grew loud as diners ordered another glass of tea or dessert and coffee. A group near the window gathered up birthday wrappings and left in a chattering troupe. A table of three businessmen stood, shook hands, and ambled outside.

"Another day," Angela said, "after he paid the hands off and drove them home, he dropped by the post office. I thought something had happened but was not sure what. I think that must have been the day he got that letter."

"What letter? One from her?"

"Not *from* her but from someone that *knew* her." Angela put her fork down with a metal-on-plate clink. "I don't think he intended to tell me."

Angela stared at Ellie, glanced across the restaurant, and continued speaking in a low voice. "He'd come back from town. We'd eaten dinner and finished up the evening chores. Since it was almost dark, we just sat out on the back stoop. Mostly we just sat until he started talking. He ranted about all the rot in the military, taking care of his friends, and how no one understands the whole war thing. He kept saying he needed to last. Not die over there. I just listened. I didn't know what else to do."

Ellie took a deep breath and let it out slow.

"Then he sort of drifted off into talking about a clinic," Angela said, "the children, wounded peasants, Viet Cong infiltrating, *and* Americans lost in the elephant grass. Mumbled about villagers, sanitation problems, and lack of supplies. Kept mentioning a woman medic."

"He never told me." Ellie frowned, crow's feet around her eyes crinkled deeper.

"Well, when he described the woman's braid, her scar, I understood he thought her special. That's when I realized he'd never *really* be home again. Never reconcile with *either* of us. Too many things, too short a time. He didn't say those things, I simply *knew* them." Angela paused and then added, "Too much has happened to everyone. Too damn fast. Stuff cuts too close to the bone."

Ellie folded her arms on the table, her face thoughtful. "You could be right. Reid didn't so much dismiss me that day in the park, as he tried to be kind. He held back. I think he was groping his way home. Or at least trying." She took another sip of tea, ran her hands up and down the sweating glass. A pool of wet spread around the glass base. "It's like he wants me, needs our marriage, our bond, but feels everything crumbling and wrong."

She stared down into her plate and continued in a soft voice. "Whatever guilt he has with all the killing in Nam—and over this woman—is crushing him. I don't know if he'll ever talk about it." Ellie twisted her wedding band, a comfort gesture whenever mulling over Reid.

"I'm exhausted. And so deeply torn between him and Diana."

"Memories crop up at the oddest times. They still knock me flat," Angela said.

"Sometimes I forget there was life before the war."

Angela folded her napkin and tucked it beside her plate. "Yes. Still, despite everything, we're family."

A few diners finished, scraped their chairs back, carefully lay money on the table, and left. Sunlight filtered through the trees outside the window, changed hues with a passing cloud and grew vibrant again as the cloud drifted on.

"We spent last night together on the beach." Ellie flushed hot at the thought.

"I heard him leave." Angela took a sip of tea, cradled the glass, and rubbed the catfish logo along its side. "I expected something."

"I'm like a moth to his flame." Ellie shut her eyes against the image of her outside light and last night's dead moths littering the porch.

"Are you sure about what's happening between you?"

"I'm sure I still have feelings for him. Love, I think. I'm also sure I can't live *with* him. We're both too changed, too damaged." Ellie wadded her napkin and placed it on the table.

Angela crossed her flatware on the plate. "I've always been angry with Daddy and Reid. But he's my brother. He taught me so much, has helped with more stuff than I can remember, but truth be told, I resented him. Sometimes I wished him gone. Then he left for Vietnam, and I kept thinking, oh Lord, don't let anything happen to him."

Ellie reached across the table and held Angela's hand.

"I don't think Daddy ever loved me," Angela said. "In fact, I don't think he loved anyone. I wished him dead. Stone cold dead. When he did die, guilt ate me inside out."

Diners finished their meals and left, the restaurant doorbell tinkling with each departure. A bus boy clanked dishes, cleared empty tables, and pushed his cart through the swinging kitchen doors.

The waitress sashayed up, took their plates, and offered dessert. They sat back in their chairs, relieved at the interruption, and smiled at the thought of a sweet. They bantered back and forth before deciding to share the house specialty, a slice of chocolate pecan pie, and coffee. While waiting, they sat silently, private thoughts rattling around in their minds.

Not until the golden-crust pie, with two forks, sat on the table and the waitress gone, did Angela's eyes fill with tears. "When Jim Guy got killed, I knew I must have sinned really bad. I still can't figure out what I did to make life stomp on me so hard."

Ellie pushed the pie aside and reached for Angela's hand. "Your daddy didn't know how to care. He was too crippled himself. And, I know without any doubt, Jim Guy loved you. Reid does too." She moved Angela's fingers as she talked, a gentle this-little-piggy-went-to-market gesture.

She had never made friends easily. Now, through Reid and the previous three years, Ellie and Angela had moved from cool to caring toward each other.

Sitting up, Angela blew her nose on the napkin and gave Ellie a weak smile. Her voice heavy, she continued, "I feel so conflicted. Everything's a jumble. I doubt myself." She sat still for a long moment. "No matter what's happened, I love my brother. I love you too. I'm glad he married you."

"Oh, Angela, me too. I'm glad we're connected. Reid loves us both, not well, but the best he knows how."

"Come on, eat some of this." Ellie nodded at the pie. "You'll feel better. Chocolate always lifts any bad mood."

Angela nodded and stuffed her napkin under the edge of her plate, and in one motion, reached for a fork.

The last of the lunch crowd left, the sound of their voices trailing behind. Bussed tables were set for evening customers. The waitress made one more pass, checked for coffee refills, and placed the bill between them.

The two women sat and sipped coffee.

Chapter 47
The Letter

August 1970

With the season ended, Reid handed out bonuses, one of several farmers who shared with their workers. Calvin stood next to him and helped distribute extra to each worker. Afterward, with the crew sitting in the truck bed, Reid drove to Willington's southside and acknowledged each person with a final wave as one by one, they climbed out at their respective stops and went separate ways.

Reid had worked the tobacco as a youngster when picking meant using a wooden sled and mule pulling the heavy loads.

The mule walked at the same speed as a man handling the leaves. At the end of two alleys, the mule was unhitched, and the brimming sled skittered to the barn for the stringers. Mule and pickers lounged in the shade and drank water until the empty sled returned. Old man Holcombe had only known this labor-intensive harvesting and never switched to using a tractor. Reid had bought a tractor and forced change. Again.

The work, sticky and dirty from early daybreak until evening down, paid workers a set wage regardless of the length of day. The bonuses, however small, made the long days less onerous.

On the way back to the farm, Reid made a right at the town's single stop light and clattered across the train tracks. He took another right at the Baptist Church, drove past the feed store, and parked at the post office. The three-room building, in the shade of an oak with limbs slumping to the ground, had once been town center. Now, it was merely a faithful servant.

When the clerk saw Reid pull up, he pushed his wire-rim glasses up on his nose, rose from his porch rocker, and ambled inside. Floorboards creaked when Reid entered the building.

A wood counter, polished by Colleton County hands from the 1870s, stretched across half the room and butted into the brass-colored mailboxes lining the remainder of the room. Wavy-glass windows along the front and at either end, offered a distorted view of the street.

"Got some foreign mail I see." The clerk smiled across the counter and handed Reid an airmail envelope. "Got a Ho Chi Minh stamp."

Reid glared at the man and picked up the thin envelope trimmed with red and blue stripes. The delicate paper crinkled with his touch.

"You in charge of monitoring my mail now?"

The man shifted slightly and placed his hands on the counter. "No. I just noticed it, that's all. Not often folks in these parts get foreign stuff."

"My business," Reid said.

"Only trying to be neighborly. Make conversation." The clerk shrugged and stacked the July issue of *Progressive Farmer*, utility bills, and shopping flyers on the counter.

Reid scooped up the stack, glanced through the bills, and the magazine. Vexed, he regarded the clerk and clumped out of the building without a backward glance or further comment.

Outside, hands shaking, he crammed the letter into his pocket.

Chapter 48
Motel Talk

August 1970

By late summer, working against the crunch of time, Diana and Ellie focused on their final report. Due in September, it required several graphs, a summary statement, and final recommendations. Although people still lived on the islands, the buildings and infrastructure had deteriorated. Ellie realized it would require a collective commitment by the people and those states directly involved—the Carolinas, Georgia, and Florida—to finalize funds and bring the buildings back into useful condition. The four states pushed their collective public relations and tourism components, but still, fell short of needed monies. The Georgia Historical Society finally identified limited construction money. The Florida highway department found road funds for connections to the Florida islands. A hodgepodge of in-kind resources and sponsorships cobbled together might swing the project from red to black. A final report reflecting local support was key to their grant application funding.

Ellie and Diana hoped the pull of history and low country cuisine might draw enough tourist dollars to boost the islands' economy—and in the process preserve sea island culture. Marketing, aimed at vacationers and out-of-state travelers, would be essential. They worked late into the evenings, fixated on completing the project.

Earlier in the week, returning from fieldwork near St. Helena Island, Ellie and Diana grabbed a fried chicken carryout, decadent feasting at its finest. At the motel, they spread out picnic style on the bed, ate, and chatted about the marshland children.

Finished, they shoved the containers aside and concentrated on the report. Raw data had to be structured and organized, sections determined, and graphics developed.

Three hours later, exhausted with their concentration, Ellie stood and stretched. "What do you say we stop for the night? We're both pretty brain dead anyway."

"Why not? We only have a few more graphs to complete."

Together they stacked grant materials on the credenza.

"Reid's home," Ellie said. "I've seen him twice. We fought both times."

Diana arched an eyebrow and begin to gather scattered food containers. "Doll, I need to take a shower. I can't think straight after these reports. Besides, I'm sweaty and I stink." She did not smile.

"You know, I really love the field work," Ellie said. "I feel alive collecting data, shifting through and analyzing it. But with Reid here, I'm distracted and torn. In fact, I'm worn completely out with guilt."

"Really? About what?"

"Him. The project. What to do about the farm and Angela." Ellie slumped on the bed.

"I didn't hear anything about us in that list."

Ellie flinched. "Oh."

Diana pushed the litter down into the basket and continued to clean up, her back to Ellie.

"We'll get this straightened out. Let me shower first. There's a solution out there someplace. For our project and for Reid."

Diana's voice had a gravelly quality to it. She surveyed the room and gathered odd remnants, tossing the greasy containers and used napkins into the trash. She put the unused honey packets aside.

"But I love you *and* Reid and don't want to hurt *either*."

"Hurt's already happened." Diana snapped, her eyes hard and narrow. "I know what I want. *You* must decide what *you* want. I'm certainly not interested in talking about you and Reid. I want to talk about *us*. Or the report." She gathered her toothbrush and paste, stomped to the bathroom, and closed the door. The shower started.

The motel room had a stale, impersonal quality. Brown striped drapes hung over the window. A Gideon Bible lay on the chest of drawers. Two cheap lamps, one with a burned-out bulb, sat on flimsy tables beside the bed. A security chain drooped against the doorframe.

Finished with her shower and wrapped in a towel, Diana stepped into the room in a cloud of steam, her skin glowing pink. She adjusted the towel and began drying her hair.

"To be honest, I never thought a man had anything to give a woman. I mean *really*, all that testosterone and bulk. They tend to grind the life right out of you.

Emotionally *and* physically." The towel fell loose. Diana flipped the dryer off, put it aside, and tied the towel around her waist. She stretched out on the bed, plump breasts falling forward, raspberry nipples erect.

"What would you know, never having tried it?"

"It's not just what happens in the sack," Diana said, "it's all the other stuff. Follow him and his career, give it all up for children, housekeeping, oh, and be sure you keep your opinions to yourself. For your information, I *have had* a round or two with a man. All that grunting and shoving. Them asking, 'was it good? Did you like it?' Him whining it's a good move for his career. I find it distasteful."

Ellie wilted. Emotional issues swamped her, left her scrambled. Even if she ignored the job issues, and potential gossip around *those kinds* of women, she doubted she had energy to manage two lovers. Especially in the South.

She held a knotty attachment for Diana and an itching sexual pull for Reid. *What did she want from Reid? From Diana? Most of all, what about herself and a career?*

Add the Holcombe family history, and the scenario took on a deeper complexity. "Natural Resources Canada offered me a consulting job." Diana tossed the towel aside and nude, swung into a sitting position before Ellie, knees touching knees.

"What did you say? Another job? When did this happen?"

"Just recently. That project's funds are solid for five years. For year one and two, I'll have to travel between Western Canada and Washington D.C. If they extend the contract, it might be longer." She paused, spoke with deliberate emphasis. "With Reid home and you undecided, I think it's a good idea I take it."

"You'd leave me?" Ellie stumbled across the words. "You know I love you." She stared at Diana, at the curve of her hips, melon-round breasts, and blonde mound.

"I know. I love you too, doll. But, all said and done, you have an emotional and legal relationship with Reid. You have a place in the community. Our relationship affects all of that. This Gullah contract depends on whether we win the grant or not. We win and only one stays as project supervisor. I need to look a bit further into the future. You do too."

"I just don't know what the hell to do."

Diana stood, her nude body still glowing from the shower, and slipped on a baggy Hawaiian shift. She sat on the edge of the bed and stroked Ellie's thigh. "Whatever you decide will wash over everyone. I want you to stay with me. I love our time reading and going to plays and hearing lectures. I love cooking together. We are simpatico. I'm sure there's a place on my new project where you can fit in. I can swing it."

"I don't want to 'fit in.' I want to earn things on my own, not depend on you. We're a team, but we're also individuals."

"You can be an individual later. Come with me now. Cut your ties here."

Ellie cocked her head at Diana. "Like you said a woman would have to do for a husband? For any man?"

Diana regarded her short nails, rough hands, and slowly, unflinching, returned Ellie's gaze.

"Angela tells me one-minute Reid talks like a crazy person, says he loves the South." Ellie's voice quivered on the edge of tears. "The next minute he calls the South a whore covered in fly-infested rot. She says he rambles on about Vietnam, his buddies, and the waste. Next minute he clams up."

Blowing her nose, Ellie crumpled the napkin, tossed it toward the trash, and continued talking. "Angela says he seems driven, hardly sleeps, works to exhaustion, and drinks too much. Sometimes she said she hears him talking late at night, like there's another person in the room."

"And you feel responsible for his hallucinations?"

"He also bought a gun."

"You think he'll harm himself or someone else?"

"Oh, my God, I don't know. I feel guilty enough without adding *that* to it." Ellie shuddered.

"Don't think about it. Think about what *you* want." Diana picked up the motel ice bucket, and in four quick steps, stood at the door. "I want a night cap. I'm getting ice." With her hand on the knob, she leaned against the open door.

The fairy-scent of mimosa floated into the room. Static night sounds grew louder. A late guest pulled into the motel lot, cut the car lights, and began to fumble around for hanging items while complaining about lack of valet service. Moths fluttered against the outside light.

"I know you've been meeting Reid. That he still attracts you." Diana's voice carried a strained quality.

"I have. And he does." Ellie began to snuff, cried soft at first, then buried her face in a napkin, tossed it aside, and dug around on the bedside table for a Kleenex. She felt like gagging. "I'm not sure what I want or what direction to take."

"I don't want to leave you, but it's a nice career move for me," Diana said. "The money is good. I need to think about myself long-term. I can't stay here and be that third leg on a triangle. I respect Angela. Even like her. I love you. But I'm in serious competition with Reid." She closed the door on her way to the ice machine.

Chapter 49
Decisions

August 1970

Ellie, down to snuffles when Diana returned with ice, gulped out her pain. "Sometimes I think Reid's here, trying and struggling. Other times I think he's still in those jungles, slopping through whatever muck they had to slosh through."

Diana drew in a deep breath and sighed, "Ellie, doll, I'm sorry. After everything's added up, I want something in my column too." She clunked the ice bucket on the table and, hands on her hips, said, "Women like me lead schizophrenic lives. I prefer a monogamous relationship. I don't plan to deny my inner self. I want a career and need to keep abreast of the latest developments in the field. I like what I do—and, if I say so myself, I'm good at it."

"You are good at your job. That's why I so love working with you. I also want a career. If we go together, we must be equals," Ellie said.

"Yeah. It's something to consider." Diana poured two vodkas, added ice cubes, and tonic, and handed one to Ellie. "Friend once told me that the best way to get over a lover was to take a long shower and fix yourself a stiff drink." She raised her glass in a toast.

Ellie's eyes widened.

"One thing for certain, you can't just hope Reid doesn't go off the deep end. He may be here, but he's not home yet. That means you and Angela. I'm odd woman out." Diana finished her vodka, made a second one, and continued brushing her hair. "At least it's easier on women to stay low than it is for gay men. Not that that matters right now."

Ellie sipped her drink. "He said they called him baby killer on his way back. He's haunted and guilty, but I sure can't be going to the jail to bail him out every week."

Diana remained silent.

"I don't want to follow you around like some shadow person either," Ellie said. "I want my own life."

Diana stopped brushing her hair. She picked up her vodka and smeared the condensation on the glass. She leaned a hip against the dresser.

"I'm down to nubbins," Ellie said.

"Emotionally or your budget?"

"Both." Ellie wiped her nose, now raw, and tossed the Kleenex away. "He's my husband. Sort of. I have a responsibility. Besides, it's mostly just DWI stuff."

"Drunk stuff escalates. Getting a gun is not good. Everything you've said leaves me out."

Ellie glared at Diana, her body languid as she breathed in Diana's essence, reflected on Reid, and recognized a pleasurable wetness rising between her legs. She considered all the beds she'd climbed into, the wine-soaked one-night stands, torrid months-long affairs, and lips kissed—both sexes. Boston had proven more than an exciting town to explore. It had opened the door to different worlds. Now it all came down to choices. Ellie drained the last of her vodka and tonic, rattled the ice cubes around, and went to take a shower.

"One other thing." Diana sat her vodka down as Ellie walked pass. "Maybe Reid wants his own life too. Maybe he *needs* his independence."

Chapter 50
An Alley Fight

July 1970

Joe wiped the survival knife, slick with blood, on the man's shirt. "You white boys think a knife's cowardly. Me, I like to be up-close. Watch a person's face, smell his breath. Knife's silent. I like that."

The man's eyes widened and then rolled back. He scrambled against the silhouette looming over him, grabbed at the hand. "Get me a doctor. I'll die if you don't."

"Ain't that what you had planned for me?"

"You sonofabitch. I don't even know you. Why'd you cut me?"

Joe's voice vibrated cold. "One thing I learned, knife needs to be handled delicate, with precision. You gonna hurt for a time but you not gonna die from that little prick. I see or hear tell you acting out though, I'll mess you permanent. You'll be a cripple." He smiled down, his features grotesque behind the head stocking, and watched the man's face change. The sour smell of fear spiraled up between them.

The thin figure rolled onto his side, clutched his belly, and allowed his pain to sob out, low at first, then in a deep whine while blood and slobber drooled onto the asphalt. He peed his khakis.

"Case you forget, you need to remember, out of all the honkeys in this old town, *I found you.* I know what you and your racist friends did. I got ways of tracking you don't even know."

Joe bent down and wiped his bloody hands through the man's hair, smiled as the man's eyes opened wider, fear shining bright. Mouth set in a hard line, Joe watched him writhe. Soundlessly, he disappeared into the alley murkiness.

For several blocks, Joe cut through the backside of town. He slipped the nylon hose from his face and dropped it in an oily puddle behind the town department store. He watched the street a few moments, stepped out, and flowed toward the light and noise of a beer joint further down the way.

Joe knew weapons. The Marines had taught him killing. The Viet Cong had taught him stealth. He had earned his manhood on his own, one-step, one insult at a time.

****

Ellie phoned Angela, briefly told her that Calvin and Mary had driven Joe to her house the previous night. Between them, they got word to Joe's friend and waited. Word came back to meet in the Beaufort railyards two night later and be prepared to leave for good.

Until the meeting, Ellie hid Joe in Beaufort. If things went awry, she was to ferry him to Mary's people on the islands.

Joe needed backup. Ellie phoned Reid. He drove the hour from Willington to Beaufort on a moon-dark Sunday night and stood splay-legged in the shadows outside Ellie's house. Her neighbors were tucked into their homes preparing for Monday and their work week.

Joe stepped out of Ellie's back door, vaulted the rear fence, slinked down the street, and slipped next to Reid in the shadows.

"You crazy sonofabitch," Reid said. "You want to get yourself strung up? Leave Mary and Calvin to face these mouth-breathing stump-jumpers alone?"

Reid turned, walked to the truck, and stepped inside. Joe slid in beside him, and they eased forward without flicking on the lights. Both sat deep in the seat, their expressions hidden in shadow.

"I'm not leaving anyone to do anything," Joe said. "I'm going north tonight and laying a trail broad enough even a blind house cat can find. They'll follow me and leave my folks alone. Anyone coming after me, play hell once I get to Detroit."

"Detroit?"

"Got brothers there that'll take my six."

"You need more than someone to watch your back. You need to stay low. What happened to Boston?"

"Leave that to me," Joe said. "VC taught me how to get close enough to smell what you ate for dinner before you even know I'm around. Bible-thumping, dough-belly, ridge runners ain't no problem. I be safe and happy in Bean Town pouring over my studies come fall."

Reid shook his head. "You're walking a thin line. Not careful and you're dead meat."

"Those hunks of lard don't have the *cajones* to do anything further," Joe said. "They'll cry-baby to the local law to do their meanness, trying to make like it 'legal.' At least in their minds."

"Those are the worse kind—they don't get their

hands dirty. Law doesn't do anything or else turns things over to night crawlers to throw down the real shit."

"I got a feller I helped out in Nam working the switch sidings near Graham, not far out of Beaufort," Joe said. "You stump-jumpers always believe each other. One you white boys tells something on one of us, everybody follows along. Even when it don't make sense, y'all follow each other, can't see the difference between one thing and another."

"You trust him?"

"Yeah. He owes me.

"He must owe you big time to lay down against his own."

"Got this gimp leg cause of him." Joe swiveled toward Reid and stared, his head cocked sideways, and then drawled, "Besides, *you're doing it.*"

Reid sat rigid and stared straight ahead. Joe smiled slightly and watched the road. The night vibrated in a labyrinth of sound.

Several houses across the tracks, a woman yelled a string of instructions into the darkness, punctuated by a slamming door. Two cats yowled in a feline duel. Snatches of music drifted across the rail yards from the nearby project apartments.

"And your folks? What's to happen to them?"

"Mamma and Pappy stay low, work with Miss Angela, Miss Ellie, and Mamma's people, things gonna work out okay. We done talked it through." Joe wiped sweat off his upper lip with his shirtsleeve.

"Watch yourself," Reid said. "You may have to leave a little skin behind. Have a chunk of pride stepped on. For God's sake, don't kill one of them rednecks.

They'll take it out on anybody they can lay hands on. They don't care. They just get riled up and want blood. Usually black blood. They consider it free."

"I'm leaving nuthin'. Especially my pride. Besides, done had a set-to with them boys." Joe's face was blank, his lips in a hard line.

Jim Guy's old truck wheezed out of town. Reid and Joe took a mile long, circuitous route to Graham clattered over the tracks, and coasted to a stop at the south end. Reid cut the lights and engine.

The slam of couplers connecting freight cars reverberated across the area. Several tracks over a train grumbled and began a slow crawl east.

Reid slid out of the truck, stepped carefully over the rails, and moved toward a double line of freight in deep shadow. Several minutes elapsed before he re-emerged and spoke in a low voice.

"Your man's here. Says he's working alone tonight, acting as brakeman. He's waiting."

Joe gave a curt nod and slid out on the passenger side. He picked up a canvas sack, slung it over one shoulder, and followed Reid.

"You travelling light. Sure this'll work?"

"I'm good. Let's go."

A man's silhouette appeared from beyond the switch signal. They could hear gravel crunch as he walked down a line of boxcars to the end. He hoisted himself onto the caboose platform, flicked his lantern on, and waved the engineer all clear. The train began a slow groan forward.

Joe scratched along his jawline, eyed Reid, and spoke slow. "For a cracker, you not bad. Times get better, maybe we sit down together with a beer."

"You not bad for a spade either. Maybe we can have two beers." Reid smiled.

"Two? Guess you'd best plan on picking up the tab." Joe laughed under his breath.

They listened to the whisper of iron-on-iron, the heavy rumble shuddering up through their soles into their knee joints. Air from the cars brushed against their faces and grew stronger with each turn of the wheels, carrying the stench of grease and oil and sweat.

"I gotta move," Joe said. "Damn train picks up speed fast once it gets started."

Reid nodded—and extended his hand.

Chapter 51
Midnight

September 1970

The sound, like pumice dust between sheets of paper, intensified.

The brass got it wrong, way wrong. They lied. Never should have been there. Even my soul has rotted.

Reid sensed the grit and noise. He pulled at his ear lobe struggling to stop the sensation. "But we're home now. We did the best we knew how."

No one hears. No one wants to know. Too many lies.

"Some hear. Some understand." Reid braced his back against the wall, gouged at his eyes with clenched fists. "Things will get better."

I needed to stay in that green hell with the others. Stay Forever.

"No. Stay with me. Don't quit. You're safe."

I can't forget.

"We did the best we knew. We tried to help." Reid unclenched his fists and dropped his hands.

We tried.

"Our best. We did our best."

The water ties us—you and me. No one dies on the beach. The godforsaken rivers stank with bodies. Bloated. Floating. No one dies on the beach. The voice

228

scratched against Reid.

"No. The rivers feed the land. They flow to the sea. They connect everything."

Water connects. Water moves. Changes constantly.

"Stay."

Angela no longer came into the kitchen to offer silent support. Maybe she never did. He couldn't remember. Breath rasped through his teeth, his heartbeat began to slow, and his hands to steady. He shivered and stumbled to the bedroom, slid into work-soft jeans, pulled on a tee, and stuffed a pack of Camels and lighter in his pocket.

He made coffee, poured a cup, and stood outside on the stoop.

A thin light crept across the sky, another hot day forming. Bugle trotted up the steps and sat next to him. Two transparent children fingered her floppy ears and giggled.

Reid pinched a cigarette between his teeth and lit up. The smoke coiled up and stung his eyes as the children dissolved into the ground fog. He sat down on the top step and stared across the farm.

She was Vietnamese, a sworn enemy. He owed her nothing. He needed to get out.

Alive.

Chapter 52
Guilty Conscience

August 1967

Reid had stopped at the clinic a second time with chocolate bars and toys. He carried several boxes inside and set them near a door he had seen the woman use.

As if summoned, Linh appeared, glanced at the cartons. Children sidled near, stared with dark eyes, and inched still closer. She gestured permission to open the boxes and take candy on top. Grubby hands plunged inside, snatching all they could carry. Like a flight of birds, they darted outside and vanished in cooking smoke and haze.

Reid watched, a slow grin creeping over him at the children's noisy excitement.

With the flurry gone, she spoke in French-accented English. "I am Vietnamese. This is *my* country where *my* ancestors live. I do not like you brutish Americans." She waved a dismissal.

He held a container of medical supplies and stared at her. "Look at these people. They're sick. You need this medicine. They're *your* people. Help them." Frowning, he sat the supplies down.

"You have no understanding." She disappeared into the tangle of huts.

He shook his head, plopped his helmet on, and

walked back to the jeep. Swinging into the driver's seat, he cranked on, and wheeled around, glancing toward the clinic over his shoulder.

She was standing in the doorway, her trousers fluttering in the slight breeze. "My name is Le Thi Linh," she said, her voice steady.

He noticed again the thin scar and the blue-black rope of hair. "I'm Reid Holcombe. From South Carolina."

Neither smiled.

****

Reid dropped by the clinic on some pretext whenever time allowed—a surplus of antibiotics, bandages from the Red Cross, candy bars, or left-over C-rations.

Each visit, he sought her out. Sometimes he waited while she made a dying man comfortable or held the hand of a woman crying. Often a nurse or two found chores in the area near Linh, as if their silent presence protected her. She distained to acknowledge him or say his name.

Once, she made smoky tea on an outside grill and allowed him to sit with her. They did not talk.

Weeks later, one evening, Reid found her in her outside area and squatted silent against the hut wall.

She did not speak.

Moans and shuffling from inside the clinic floated gossamer gray around them. A child cried, a tired wail. Somewhere a phlegmy cough rose wet, then quieted. A vehicle grunted pass, punctuating the humid dusk with diesel fumes.

He stood, paced back and forth, spoke in an angry tone, rambling on about his tobacco farm, life before the war, and the sea that washed against both shores.

She did not respond.

He spoke of men blown into chunks, his bowel-loosening fear of mortar attacks, and the screams of the wounded. He talked of his adrenaline-high in battle.

She listened without expression, with no show of emotion, nor response. Despite limited English, the tone of the words rang clear.

****

Reid was no stranger to the brutality of Marines when the villages were ransacked—the rice scattered, water buffalo and pigs slaughtered, and huts set ablaze. And the rape. He struggled to block images and refused to verbally acknowledge the atrocities. He reasoned that his pseudo protection of her clinic with medicines, food, and hospital supplies, whitewashed all things.

Late one afternoon, before Têt feasts, she made love to him for the first time, her way of paying for the clinic supplies and his unfocused eye. Since destiny had placed them on opposite sides of a cultural divide, it seemed prudent to utilize what fate offered.

Sexual favors were the two-sided coin of the day, the only value with which she leveraged additional favors and tied him to her and, by extension, to her clinic and cause. She appeared to hold part of herself in reserve in order to tolerate his touch. He had no such reservation.

Afterwards, when they finished, she dressed quickly, and, without saying more, went her separate way.

Gradually, the Year of the Monkey 1968 emerged.

****

Linh gave the Viet Cong, anonymous figures in

black, information, ammunition, and medicine while she doled out local intelligence on munition caches and supply routes to the South Vietnamese Army. Frustrated U.S. troops, caught between VC and ARVN, tried to decipher their tangled circumstances.

A gaming chip, Linh was unofficially used by all sides. She quietly realized the end would come in time.

The war, with attack and counterattack, horror and kindness, retribution and absolution, shifted daily. Although Linh acknowledged her dead parents and husband, wore a white mourning band, and burned Buddhist incense, her prayers were for her ravished country. Only she and her brother remained.

Her ragged feelings grew deeply layered, had trembled somewhere between kindness and revulsion. For her, the differences in men began and ended with their uniforms. Reid included.

Chapter 53
The Sale

September 1970

The front door clicked closed, the room quiet. The striped cat, sphinxlike under a chair, stared. Angela slumped down at the kitchen table.

Reid stood, hands in his pockets, and listened to Ollie Jacobson's pickup rattle down the driveway. Three weeks had dissolved from the time he called, dropped by the farm, and put a buy offer on the table.

Small town grapevines ran deep and fast, whether good news or bad. Ollie knew of the Holcombe setbacks and gradual spiral into debt. Farmers recognized among themselves, a shared love of land, plants, and animals. Profit motives lurked, but the first criterion was land stewardship.

Ollie and Jim Guy were friends, having met at county gatherings. They talked best farming practices, tobacco prices, and advocated with county extension agents and Farm Bureau during coffee shop klatches. Several weeks after Jim Guy was killed, Ollie offered to buy the farm. Big tobacco had also made an offer.

Angela responded to the offer in a dry, direct tone. "Reid's half owner. I've got to work things out with him. The bank carries the loan on this place, so they'll have to be part of any sale also."

Months earlier, Ollie had found Angela milking Pansy and leaned on the fence talking while she finished.

"Never expected stuff to end up like it has," she said. "Me and Calvin will work the place till Reid gets home. I appreciate the offer, but I have to wait. Besides, I don't know what I want to do yet."

Milk sloshed out of the pail when she walked to the house. The cats, looking for their handout, followed.

****

When Reid returned from Nam, Ollie offered again to buy the homeplace.

Reid had been furious. "The gall of him, a tobacco farmer from the north of the county, offering to buy a farm three generations Holcombe."

He had stayed at the Blue Star late into the night and refused to discuss any possible sale with Angela. He called Ellie, then hung up when she answered. He trooped back to the farm at daylight, having slept in the truck in the parking lot.

Other nights spent at the Blue Star, morphed into a haze of vomit and sour beer. He sweated out his headache and hangover working the fields, helped with evening chores, and then repeated the cycle. His Clemson deputy friend, unable to run cover any longer, arrested Reid to keep him out of trouble whenever he found him trying to drive or asleep in some parking lot.

After the bar confrontation, Angela had put Jim Guy's truck up as bond. Reid sagged in shame.

Leaving the jail, Ellie and Angela held hands, the only comfort available. They arranged themselves in the front seat of Ellie's station wagon. Reid silently climbed in the rear.

They drove forty miles from Beaufort to the farm and sat around the kitchen table silent while Ellie made coffee.

In the end, the bartender's advice had pushed Reid. "Cut bait, leave it all. Marriage happens to be the main reason for divorce anyway. Besides, families get too complicated. *Find your peace first.*"

Later Angela, her face stiff with concentration, stated the obvious. "We have no choice. We have to sell. Ollie's a good man. He's a fine farmer. Cares for the land. We'll be okay with him owning the place. Besides, he was Jim Guy's friend."

By dawn, through osmosis, they accepted the inevitable: their world had changed.

Reid stepped up. "I'll call that blood-sucker Cavanagh and make an appointment at the bank and arrange for Ollie to come down to the real estate office. I'll get any lawyer we might need and finalize everything. We'll both sign off on details." Reid smiled faintly. He started out but paused and stopped slightly behind Angela's chair, placed his hand on her shoulder. She laid her head on his hand for a long moment and patted him gently. "Things will work out."

He squeezed her, his voice husky. "Yeah, Sis. Things will work out."

Reid stopped next to Ellie, wrapped his arms around her, and held her, kissed her on the cheek, and walked out. She silently fingered her wedding band.

In a gesture of friendship, Ollie Jacobson deeded three acres and the house to Angela. He grumbled good-naturedly saying, "Who would want that crippled mule and those damn useless cats?"

Chapter 54
Tobacco Auction

September 1970

Reid and Angela trucked the last bales of tobacco into auction, one final effort to end up in the black for the year. They off-loaded the harvest and stood near the warehouse entrance watching the buyers walk up-and-down the aisles handling and smelling the tobacco leaves, bidding, and moving on. Capitol for the next year's work was made or lost with this dance of men among the bales. Women, often the backbone of labor, stood in silent groups near the doors, faces drawn and worried.

The Holcombe family had a reputation among buyers for high-grade bright leaf, cured to a delicate bronze with leaf moisture to keep the leaves doe-soft and pliable. No mold. Their carefully stacked sheets contained clean leaves throughout, without trash hidden between layers.

Reid often acknowledged his father's acumen with growing and curing tobacco and his status as an auction house favorite.

Nights while in Nam, Reid lit a cigarette, savored the mild taste, and decided it must be Holcombe tobacco. If not Holcombe grown, then at least a Carolina producer. He'd watch smoke coil up in pearl-gray spirals, elongate, and dissipate in flat ribbons.

As kids, they had delighted in puffing breath into the air pretending they were smoking while chasing the condensation. Ellie had been fond of saying those spirals were the soul in suspension, visible only when smoking a cigarette or in frigid weather.

With the last "sold American" shout from the auctioneer, Reid and Angela climbed in the truck and started home. Saturated, end-of-season markets had left little room for profit.

Angela broke their silence, her voice calm as if simply thinking aloud. "I accepted another contract for the school year yesterday. They'll let me teach one art class for juniors. It's an elective. No telling how it will go."

Reid nodded, eyes fixed on the road.

"Naturally, they added math and algebra. Stuck in girls' gym too. Couldn't let me get away with a light load." She shrugged.

"You be okay with that?" Reid watched her face. It crumpled slightly and then grew blank.

"I love my art. That was Mother's gift. I'm still learning, moving from watercolors to acrylics. I'll be fine." She fumbled a moment trying to roll the truck window down, cursed under her breath, got it adjusted, then sagged back in the seat.

"I guess all said and done," she said, "I have to thank the Old Man for putting grit in my craw. He had a damaged heart, no love in it, but he taught me to be tough."

Reid snorted. "Yeah, tough. No feelings."

She sat quiet a few minutes, then continued talking. "Did I tell you Mary Terrell got a letter from Joe? He made it to Boston. Says he'd like to come home again, but not until the South makes changes. Big changes."

Reid's face relaxed as if an image had materialized on the dashboard. He grinned. "He's a good man."

"What with the farm going to Ollie, I'll try my hand at a little market gardening. I've hired Calvin and put him on a regular salary. Not much, but it's year-round." Angela chuckled. "He says salary's real status for him. Keeps him from depending on tobacco. Especially since he's getting older."

"Terrells are good people. Calvin will be a fine hand.

Angela fell silent.

Grateful for the lull, Reid allowed himself to drift. Time became jumbled, grew fragile, formed crusty scabs. Têt Offensive. Cambodian bombings. Farms sold. Families scattering. Helicopters. Chicago Seven. Cigarette ads banned.

He needed to settle things with Ellie. Her job and the house were secure, but their emotional connection fluttered like a plastic bag, snagged on fencerow weeds, and ripped apart.

He drove, a peace settling between him and his sister. She'd held the farm together despite their father for the time he had been at college, through the months of basic training, and, finally, his Nam years.

Giving her his share of the homeplace seemed right. Especially since he did not want to farm. She loved the land, the seasonal cycles, the plants and animals. As a widow, she couldn't work the larger farm alone. The deeded acreage would be enough. Content to teach math, girls' gym, one art class, and fool around with market gardening, Reid understood Angela was settled, at least as much as possible.

He still needed to buy wheels but with no job, no credit, and limited funds, it was not time to get picky. He'd buy whatever used car he could afford outright.

The question of *his* peace hovered untethered.

****

The tobacco harvest paid off part of the farm debt and lawyer's fees. By the time equipment, some of the livestock, and most household items were auctioned, Reid and Angela were able to pay off back taxes. To turn the farm over to another person hurt something deep inside, left Angela despondent, and Reid empty, despite his dislike for farming.

His future bristled, wrapped him with razor wire.

Figures, wearing white crepe headbands, danced alongside the truck as he drove toward the farm. They hovered, trailing disembodied voices that chanted of a rising moon. He willed his ears deaf, a useless gesture from his little boy self—if he could not hear a bad thing, he'd be safe.

"September," he said aloud. "All things change in September."

Chapter 55
An Invitation

September 1970

Reid parked down the street from Ellie's house. A feeling of *déjà vu* settled as he remembered the first time he and Ellie strode along the cracked sidewalk and climbed the worn steps.

They had met the landlord, an older fellow with a cane. Ellie gushed with plans for painting the rooms, changing out the kitchen fixtures, and adding throw rugs—already making the place theirs even before they signed a rental agreement.

He had poked around in the weedy yard. The luxury of sweating while pushing a hand mower appealed to him. He noticed the picnic table, the shade trees, and the rickety privacy fence with missing boards. The house, albeit a rundown rental, their first together adventure. They plotted over beers and pledged sweat equity in exchange for lower rent. They listed repairs, scrutinized their budget, and decided to adopt a dog. Together, they started homemaking—until the war had washed over them and left them gasping for breath.

Reid stood in the yard. A faint glow through the gauzy curtains gave off an aura of coziness. Moths fluttered around the porch light, drawn by something known only to them. In the morning, they'd be dead. He climbed the steps and knocked on the screen door.

Ellie answered. A soft halo outlined her body. "Reid. What are you doing here?"

He shivered and stared at her short jean skirt, hair pulled into a casual wad behind her neck, and that scattering of freckles. He swallowed.

"Thought you might like to drive out to the beach. Have a beer." Long neck bottles clinked as he held up a six-pack. "I bought an eggbeater off the used car lot yesterday. Didn't have quite enough cash though."

"What did you do?"

"Talked the dealer into taking my gun in trade. I'm naked again."

She stood with her mouth open. "Sounds like a sensible trade. Besides, there's nothing here to shoot."

He focused on the street. A kid on a bike whirred past. Dogs yapped in the neighboring yard. Down the block someone slammed a car door.

Reid turned back to Ellie and grinned. "You can be my first passenger." He gestured toward the coupe with its rust-coated front wheel-well and hail-pocked body.

"Used to be Corvair had style—for a compact, that is. Then nobody wanted them because of some handling or braking mess. Got voted worse car of 1961."

"No wonder the dealer took your gun."

"Yeah." Reid reflected quietly, shrugged, and continued. "Don't go casting off on my new wheels. Just look at that sloped rear end—it's got energy to burn." He mimicked the downward look with his hand. "Those dents scream energy for sure."

"Energy that'll make any small-town cop around here grab their ticket book the minute you drive by,"

Ellie said.

She stepped out onto the porch. The screen door slapped closed behind her. "What a compliment. An in-person visit from the star of the county jail with a second-hand car ride as a peace offering." Hair along her arms prickled, she shivered, and thought *stud muffin.*

He rattled the bottles again. "Come on. Don't tease. Help me with these. Lone Star. National Beer of Texas. Our brew. Bought them special. Besides, night's cool and everything's sold."

"Sounds promising. What else?"

"I'm ready to talk." He scrutinized her face. "And *listen.* What about you? You got a helluva lot to answer for too."

She took several steps, curled her bare toes off the edge of the porch, and tried to decipher his thoughts. Finally, with a quick motion, she rubbed her forehead and spoke in a crisp voice. "Diana's here. She's packing her final things. I'll tell her goodbye and that we're headed out." She paused with her hand on the handle. "Want to meet her?"

"Meet her?"

Ellie shrugged. "Why not?"

"What do you think? Meet the lesbian that's doing you? Doing it so good I'm left in the dust? Helluva of world, ain't it?"

"Shall I take that as a 'No'?"

He shifted the six-pack, frowned at her.

"This is my choice, my life," Ellie said. "You can respect that, or you can fight me. Especially since I'm not the same person you married. Some things change. Some never do."

"You're damn right things change. I don't want to get the hell started on changes. Things that never were and never can be. Nothing is the same."

"I'll take that as a 'hell no.'"

The neighborhood vibrated with life. Boys played ball, drifted up and down the alley. Cooking odors wafted out. Evening TV flickered through the windows, rooms glowing blue. Sounds of a working-class neighborhood in action.

Reid looked at the street again, its purple shadows and cloistered families. "You're right—it's hell no. I'll pass on that handshake. Let's take care of one thing at a time."

They climbed into the faded Corvair, he cranked the engine, and they rattled off toward the bay. Twenty minutes later, they swung off the highway and drove down a sandy track toward McKenzie's Point, a spit of land that protruded into the sea. She rolled her window down, relaxed against the slow breeze. He lit a cigarette. They drove in silence.

At the end of the track, he cut the engine, crushed his cigarette in the overflowing ashtray, opened the door, and got out. He sat on the sand, took off his tennis shoes, and dug his feet into the warmth left over from the day.

She sat next to him and slipped her sandals off. "Humm. Feels good."

They stood, placed their shoes on the car hood, and side by side jogged along the tide line. Foam-crested ripples splashed up their legs. With the summer crowds gone, the area had a pleasant, deserted quality.

A hundred yards down, breath coming in labored gasps, they slowed and ambled toward the long finger of land jutting toward the coastal islands.

Sea oats grew sparse across the beach and anchored it, all the while bending their tall stems in the wind. The sun dipped, throwing its last light through foaming sun-sprays. A summer fire ring stood yards above tideline with a driftwood tree trunk. The surf rose and receded, then rose and receded again under a salty, adventuring wind.

Before he shipped, they had often sat together in this same spot in those days between boot camp and specialized training, propped against the same driftwood tree. They had stared at the stars and talked over their plans for his return home when they could start graduate school, buy a house, live the good life. Circumstances had eroded those dreams.

Propped against the bare tree, legs stretched out, Reid lit up a smoke. He clicked the lighter closed and sat quiet a long moment. "I've been thinking," he said, "I'm not going to file for divorce. You want one, you file. You're still on my next of kin papers so I'm okay with whatever."

She cocked her head, stared at him.

"Remember, if anything happens, as my wife you can use any of my military benefits. Got rights to any inheritance too. You may need them. Besides, why let stuff go to waste?"

"What does that mean?"

"You never know. Things happen." His voice trailed off as he squeezed her hand and kissed her fingertips. She mirrored the gesture.

Chapter 56
Decisions

September 1970

Silent, Ellie and Reid listened to the ocean's swoosh and savored the salt-laden air. Finally, Reid stood and pulled Ellie to standing. They strolled back.

At the car, Reid tossed their shoes into the car and took out the six-pack of Lone Star and gathered a frayed quilt from the floorboard.

He sprawled on the windward side of a dune, spread the tattered coverlet, and set the beer next to him.

She stretched out alongside.

They had first discovered Lone Star beer on a visit to Fort Worth, Texas when, on a whim, they had driven south to see the winter fat livestock show. Once settled into Motel 6, they spent their time groping each other rather than walking the fairgrounds in the February cold. Several days later, satiated and too sore to continue in the motel room, they wandered among the cattle exhibits, strolled up and down the historic stockyard boardwalk, and ate tacos. Reid bought a Stetson and Ellie opted for a plaid, western-cut shirt with pearl snaps. She joked, saying she should wear it on the beach instead of a bikini top, the shirt tails knotted under her breasts.

They had driven back to Beaufort arriving a few hours before Reid reported for special training. In honor of that trip, Longneck Lone Star had continued to be their favorite. He opened a brew, offered it to her, and opened one for himself. They drank. He watched pinpricks of starlight flicker like fireflies across the sky. Tracer rounds ignited the cosmos.

He cleared his throat and said, "Now that me and Angela have the tobacco and the farm sold, I'm leaving."

"Leaving? What are you going to do?" Ellie asked.

"Hauled the last of our crop down to Georgia, almost broke even. At least for this year." He gestured toward the car. "Just look at this fine example of my profits. Corvair. Used. No debt, no payments. Kinda like us, unsafe at any speed." He leaned back, and scooped up a handful of sand, allowed the grains to trickle through his fingers.

"Angela says she'll go back to teaching. She'll try her hand at market gardening. Calvin will work too. Things might change later."

"I didn't ask about the tobacco. Didn't ask about Angela. I asked what *you* are planning. *You.*"

"Hell, woman, I can't rightly say. I'm not here. I'm not in Vietnam. I'm not with you. I don't have a place. Everybody's gone. Things are too mixed up." Holding the beer bottle neck, he stared across the sand. "I can't even organize."

"What else?"

"In Nam, I was unit point man. I feel better when I'm moving. When I'm alone."

"I know we were never right for each other," she said. "We got married because we both needed something. I'm not sure what I wanted when we tied the knot. Whatever it was, it almost worked."

"I think it did work," Reid said. "I've had you and I've had other women. Each woman has been good. In different ways. I've learned from every one of you." He wiped sand off his hand. "But you...you hold my heart. Just you."

Ellie smiled at him. "Stuff only seems to make sense when you look back. I think some people are meant to leave home, find a new place. Others do better staying put."

"Kinda like the song—a wandering soul or heart at rest." He raised his beer, toasted the purple line dividing earth and sky, and gulped the last swallow.

"Ellie, I love you. *Love. You.* What people say when they are together grunting in the dark doesn't usually hold up in daylight." He shook his head. "With you, *it held.*"

"Once I loved you too." She rested her head on his shoulder, hands encircled his arm, and fingers laced tight. "Maybe I still do. But we're different. The old time-and-change thing happened to both of us."

Reid's hard form shuddered. "You hurt me. Bad. Still hurts." He stuck his empty bottle back in the carton.

"I hurt too," Ellie said. "I died every day, just a little. I felt abandoned, tossed away. When you lose someone, no matter how, you remember things before the loss. You remember what made you laugh, what hurt."

"Difference is I still love you," Reid said. "You're like a hairball I've choked on. Hair and slobber galumphed together in a wad on the floor. The kind of thing you step on at night going to the can."

"That sounds plain nasty." She laughed, until she snorted, then picked at the damp bottle label, peeled it off tatter by tatter, and sloshed the last of her beer around.

"I used to think it was only lust I felt for you. Now I know there were deeper roots between us. Seems like everything's the same and yet everything's different." She leaned forward and spoke rapid fire. "But I also relish my work with the Gullah. I respect those people and their culture. I need my own paycheck. Feels good making decisions and doing research."

"Whoa, baby." He sat up and motioned slow down. "Let me catch up." He held her above the elbows, kissed her cheek, her neck, her eyelids. "What happens to that lesbian Diana?"

Ellie took a deep breath. "I don't know. I never intended to fall in love with her. It simply happened. She was hot. I was lonely. We liked the same things. Talked a lot. Doesn't matter now."

"Because of me? Too much stud to leave?" He grinned and cocked an eyebrow.

"No. No," Ellie said. "Well... maybe. A little. She's taking a job in Canada. She'll be working on some project in the Yukon. Too much has happened to her and me. Too much to both of us." She watched the sea a moment, sighed, and continued. "I don't think she and I were meant to last. We were both crossing from one stage to another, deciding on directions. I waited until you got back. I didn't want to tell you in a letter."

"The 'Dear John' thing? Or should I say, 'Dear Jill'?"

"Like that." Ellie sat quiet, her eyes flickering

across the sea. "Didn't seem right to do anything before you got back. I needed to see you before I made any decision."

Reid frowned and sat legs crossed, hands dabbling in the sand. "I'm back, she's gone, and no one gets the brass ring. Helluva world."

She saw the groove between his eyes smooth and the taut line of his mouth softened. She dropped her bottle into the cardboard holder with a clink.

"You see, I thought if I married, put on a respectable face, it'd all be okay. Can't beat nature though. Your own or theirs. Folks get scared of anything different."

"Damn right." He scratched the stubble along his jaw and then ran his hand through his hair.

They sat silent. A breeze sighed, salt and time riding on it. The ocean whispered, a constant breathing in and out.

Ellie broke the silence, her face toward the water. "Diana leaves next Thursday for DC then Canada."

Reid cocked an eyebrow. "That means what?"

"I'll stay, continue my work with the Gullah. Eventually get a graduate degree. Be my own person, take ownership of myself. You coming home pushed me to decide."

"Yeah? Ownership? That's a good word. So, everyone's going separate ways?"

"Not exactly. We'll just give each other room. We'll stay connected but be our own persons too."

"Still sounds to me like everyone's going separate ways." Reid leaned back, started to light a cigarette, thought better of it, stuffed the pack back into his pocket, and instead repeated, "Separate ways.

Ownership. Self." He rubbed the days-old growth of stubble, heard the paper crinkle of it.

"I guess, in a nutshell. Separate ways."

They sat, their bodies warm against each other. Sea grass trembled in the wind as grains of sand lifted from the dune, stinging as it blew pass toward another place.

"Seriously, what do you plan?"

"I'm not sure. Find myself—or at least find a place I can be content. Take responsibility for my destiny. I've got a lot to untangle."

"I loved you once. Maybe I still love you. We're both kind of lost, on paths different than we planned. Do you think we'll reconnect?"

"Reconnect. Sounds good, but I don't know." Reid stroked her face with work-rough hands, trailed his finger along her lips. "I'll be fine. But I lied. I need to tell you one more thing." He leaned over and picked up another bottle, opened it, and handed it to her.

Ellie took a gulp of beer. "What?"

Chapter 57
Confession

September 1970

"There was a woman. In Nam," Reid said. "Without her I don't think I would have made it."

"A woman? What the hell?"

"A Vietnamese woman. A country medic." He dangled his beer bottle between two fingers. "It was an accident. We drifted together. I thought she'd come back with me." Reid stared down the beach, watched a woman in an *áo dài* top, braid slung across her shoulder, strolling toward them. He trembled, felt sweat beads form across his forehead.

Ellie glowered at him. "How dare you judge me, you prick." She leaned forward and delivered a hard, full-hand face slap.

His head snapped to the side. Reid grabbed Ellie's wrist, watched her eyes narrow.

She stared at the red imprint of her hand. "You had your own 'Dear John' ready. That's a tad hypocritical. What were you planning? An international stable?"

"Fuck you. Me living on a razor blade. Men around me splattered into brains and gristle. Those screams. The smells." He released her arm, got up, paced toward the high tide mark and back, and then stopped in front of her, snarling spittle and words into her face. "*Double* fuck you. You were safe. You don't know what the hell it was like."

She slung her bottle at him, the gold and red and white logo spinning, beer splattering as the brown bottle bounced off his chest and rolled across the sand.

"Before you think harsh of me, I wasn't looking." Eyes wide, Reid thrust his face toward her, breathing hard, then lowered his gaze, and dropped down in the sand. His shoulders slumped. "Things got messed up too fast. Friends shot to hell. Brass pulling their puds."

"So, what was she? A bar whore or what?"

"No." He leaned back on his elbows, faced the open sea. "She worked a clinic outside Saigon. My unit helped them a couple of times. Helped when villagers got shot up and needed medical attention. We adopted that clinic as part of a med-cap program, a sister hospital." He stared off, sounds of mortar fire ringing around him. He shook his head.

"We talked a few times, especially late, when things got quiet. At least, I talked. She listened." A man in green camouflage and a small boy crept up the dune and sat on the quilt. The boy giggled. Reid rubbed his eyes, shoved the gauzy figures away, and stared down at his broken fingernails and work-cracked hands. "We made love, but she didn't love me. We used each other."

Ellie sat stiff; her hands fisted.

"We both needed comfort, something beyond the war. One day I'd be out blowing peasants to hell and the next saving them at the clinic." Reid stared off into space, wrung his hands, and shook his head again.

"What did you plan for me?" Ellie hissed, her eyes narrowed.

"Never figured that out. I thought she'd be different."

"Based on what?"

He planted his feet in the lacy foam and watched as swells rose and rolled inland.

Abruptly, he whirled around toward Ellie and flashed a wicked grin. "Let's go swimming!" He peeled off his clothes, and naked, splashed into the surf and disappeared.

She scrambled to her feet, called him, and ran toward the water. She ripped at her shirt, hollered, waded into the water in her skirt, and dove into a wave; her arms sliced through the sea. Water pearls dripped from her hands as she swam.

She slowed, bobbed, and scanned for Reid. Unable to see him, she twisted around and around, called his name. Sea swells rose and splashed against her face. Gagging, she swam further out, ducked under the brine, and bobbed up paddling, screaming his name over and over.

From underwater, his hands encircled her waist and pulled her toward him. He surfaced laughing.

Grabbing his neck, she wrapped her legs around him, kissed with all the passion of empty nights and missed letters. She stroked his face, kissed again, and savored the essence of beer and cigarettes. She slipped her panties off, allowed them to float away. Like river otters, they spun in tight circles twisting, laughing, and scissor-kicked to stay afloat. She felt him stiff against her.

"Goddamn it all. I pick women that already love something more than me." He stroked her breasts, felt the nipples grow hard, and fondled her mound.

Still kicking in circles, he loosened her arms from his neck, held them down against her body, caressed her wet hair, released his hold, and began a slow crawl to shore.

Gasping, she stared after him, bobbed a few times, and followed, her strokes muscular and eager.

On the shore, he knelt in the surf's edge, waited until she stood before him, and pulled her to kneeling. He kissed her and fondled her small breasts while she pulled her shirt up and braced on her hands and knees. He entered her darkness, his balls thumped against her round buttocks while her hips ground into him. He thrust until his member erupted and her cat's yowl of pleasure vibrated into the dark. He kissed her and slid off, breathing heavy. Spent, they lay silent, side by side, and sorted through the debris of their dreams.

Chapter 58
The Beach

September 1970

A bored fingernail moon stared at the two figures on the beach with their timeworn drama. The sea grew quiet, curled lazily while one foam-laced ripple dissolved into another and another and scattered down the beach.

Reid pulled the wet tee over his head and shivered at the dampness. He stepped into his gritty jeans, zipped them closed before sprawling on the frayed quilt next to a clump of beach grass.

Ellie shook sand from her blouse, struggled with two missing buttons, and twisted her skirt back into place. She ignored the lost panties.

He popped a beer for himself, offered her one, and watched as she finger-combed her hair. They drank in silence, each acutely aware that time had grown short, decisions needed to be made, and trust shared. Sea sounds, at once soothing and savage, filled the void between them.

Ellie, staring straight ahead, spoke first. "You're a hypocrite, too. You've got no room to point fingers at me and Diana. You never said anything about that woman."

"I know." He took a cigarette out of his pants and

thumped it against his lighter. "Didn't want to tell you in a letter. No 'Dear Jill.' I've got my standards too."

He flipped the lighter open, lit up, and clicked it closed. He cupped the tip of his cigarette in his hands, hid the bright glow, took deep a drag, and exhaled. "Chinese filtered into the Nguyen dynasty centuries ago. They are the ones that forced the French abdication and started that bloody damn civil war. Then here we come, men-boys strutting along, waving guns, ready to save the world from Communism."

Face taut with concentration, he ached to have her absolve him. "Once when I was at Vung Tau, I stood out in the surf, just stood there. Every time a wave lapped against me, *I felt you*."

Unlike Saigon, Vung Tau was pleasant, alternating from milky-white temperatures to tangerine warmth. Tropical colors splashed long ago on the colonial buildings accented their graceful archways and carved façades. Here and there, gray mold crept down the walls. Memories of sugar-textured sand, mango trees, and amber rivers scrolled before him. Streets glistening with rain, lazed in a musty matrix. Reid took a last drag and flicked the cigarette away, waited until the glowing arc disappeared.

"What was her name?" Ellie asked.

"Linh. It means gentle spirit or soul." He scratched Le Thi Linh in the damp sand with his finger. "Seemed an odd name for her. She had a puckered scar through her eyebrow, not big, only a sliver. She never explained how she got it."

Silent, Ellie waited for him to continue.

"Vietnam was not one thing. Saigon especially. It had those big old boulevards, sleazy bamboo-bars,

Catholic schools, and those kids in neat uniforms. Of course, there was all that political stuff—assassinations, monks on fire, hit and run stealing—mixed in. Motorbikes everywhere. They were like a Greek chorus."

He sat still as if seeing a matinee from some previous time. When he spoke again, his voice deepened. "Outside Saigon, it was a whole different story. You got heat and leeches and blood-soaked mud. Adrenaline high. Noise was different, too. Choppers. Gunfire. Grenades. And the screams."

"But you fell in love."

"Yes. No. Maybe. I respected her. At least, I think I did." He erased the name with his hand and leaned back on his elbows. "She wore her hair braided in a long rope, would flip it across her shoulder. Whatever kid she was carrying would hold that braid, a comfort thing. You know, like a favorite blanket. She was a sucker to help those children." He gestured vaguely with his hand.

"What did you want from her?"

"I wanted something to be *right*. I wanted her to *forgive* me for the deaths, the waste. I wanted your replacement."

Ellie, silent, drew her knees up and rested her chin on their knobby hardness, listened to the relentless movement of the ocean.

"Sometimes," he said, "I felt we reenacted the war with our nights together. We had tender moments, but mostly not. I ended up with guilt, blacker guilt, and then more guilt piled on top. Even with her, I felt you, thought you." He stared off, held his beer bottle by the neck, allowed it to swing slightly.

With darkness, a wind gust moved across the water. Ellie shivered.

"The whole godforsaken place was collapsing, an endless hotspot," Reid continued. "I thought it was settled. Linh was to head to Thai Bay, then on to the Philippines. I'd told her what to do, how to arrange things. Like carry Buddhist papers and another set as Catholic."

His voice took on a gruff edge. "Her brother was a clever sonofabitch. He worked both sides. Couldn't trust him, but he knew how to manipulate the bureaucracy. I told them to go to Clark airbase. I'd help from there." He drank slow, finished the beer, and replaced it in the carton.

"Didn't happen. At the last minute, she stayed with that damn clinic. Her brother got a message to me. Said she wouldn't leave her ancestors, their graves needed care, they had to be remembered. Most of all, he said she couldn't leave the party. Can you believe? Couldn't leave the commies, the Party."

"Then what?"

"Her brother went on out. He could see changes coming. He wrote later. They came in and shot her. One clean bullet. Behind the ear."

"But you tried to help her."

"In a way. She kept my humanity from completely scabbing over. She let me talk." Silent, he dug his fingers into the sand, and folded inward on himself. When he spoke, his voice had a bewildered quality. "She was right about one thing. War swallows us, strips everything down to our bones. In the end, there are no winners."

Ellie studied his profile. He did not look at her but

clasped his hands on his stomach and sat legs crossed.

Reid spoke in a colorless voice. "Our troops left wounded civilians. Or commies. No one ever knew which was which.

"Clinic supplies got dropped off. We suspected she sent part to the guerillas, traded with ARVN, and used the rest for peasants. Young boys treated at her clinic got patched up, drifted away, and joined nationalist fighters.

"Not until later did I find out VC used her clinic as an ammunition drop. She used me."

He dug a hole next to his hip, stopped, and pushed sand into the hole, refilling it. "I used her."

Ellie sucked in her breath. "Used? How?"

"The whole thing was humanitarian and sabotage. Brass said to leave her smokescreen up. Even the spooks couldn't tell. They only speculated. We—me included—picked up snippets of information on VC movements and fed in erroneous intel. He glanced at Ellie, a sad smile playing along his mouth. "Kept everything in balance."

His face grew gray, furrowed with lines, and his voice dropped into a hoarse whisper. "Those people scared me. Never knew what they were thinking. One-minute okay, the next they'd blow you to hell. Sneaking around in black pajamas. All those yellow faces the same."

"Like they say about blacks?"

"Yeah, like that." He gouged at his eyes, knuckles twisting around. He stopped abruptly.

"No. Not like that. But sort of. I killed everything at one time or another, did mean, senseless things."

His voice fell another notch, scratched up his throat

in painful syllables. "Now *beings, ghosts* materialize around me, touch me, and finger my clothes, my hair. Especially at night. They watch me."

"But you felt something for this woman. This Vietnamese *person.*"

He swallowed, his Adam's apple sliding up and down. He wiped his nose with the palm of his hand and rubbed it down a pant leg.

"I'm the one that fingered her officially. ARVN would have ignored her since they used her too. But our brass wouldn't let it go. If only she had left like I told her." He grasped his stomach, bent double, and cried.

Ellie heard him gasp for air and pull himself into a tight wad of man-flesh. Mucus and tears dripped onto his chest.

She knelt beside him, petted his face, put her arms around him. She hummed and rocked.

He sobbed until he had dry heaves, and slowly, slowly relaxed into her gentleness. After long minutes, he slumped against her breasts, wiped his cheeks, and smeared hands across his shirt. His breathing finally steadied. He sprawled, head bent into her softness, hand resting on her thigh.

She leaned over, took the cap off another beer, and handed it to him.

He coughed, rolled to sitting, and let the bottle dangle between his fingers.

"Early mornings, when it was quiet and peaceful with the light through the leaves, it was like a postcard. I could have stayed forever. When things got hot, I lived on adrenaline, *thrived* on it. Out in the field, shooting, getting shot at—it was a high." He shook his head and swigged his beer. "Greatest I've ever had. Got to the point I *missed* it. Still do."

"Miss what?"

"The adrenaline. The high. Like a drug. I *needed* it."

He stretched his legs out, unzipped his jeans, and reached for her, pulled her until she rolled against his hip. She fumbled with her skirt, straddled his crotch, and pressed her hips against him. He rubbed back and forth against her warmth, his member wet and slick. He held her hips, felt her against him, legs squeezing as he pushed inside.

Kissing with a lost tenderness, they moved together, and built to an apex. Then, wordless, they sprawled beside each other, hands entwined, and listened to the sea sob.

After a time, she rolled to sitting, picked up a circular metal top. "Here's a keepsake." She kissed him tenderly.

"A Lone Star bottle cap." He stared down at the red star logo, closed his fist around the metal, and slipped it into his pocket.

"To help you remember our beach coupling."

"Couplings. Plural." A deep ache bloomed inside his chest, exploded. He sucked in his breath. Never again would they be the same. Never again would the world be in this place.

They shared the last beer, passed it back and forth, and listened to the waves until the wispy fog dissolved into a new day. Piping plovers scurried in the surf, busy with their work. Gulls squawked rude and circled overhead, demanded handouts.

He picked up a purple coquina shell, a fragile porcelain-like thing, rolled it around in his palm, and handed it to Ellie.

She stared at the tiny remnant of a life. "Purple. That's the Christian color of royalty and mourning. What now?"

"I think I'll drive down to the Glades," Reid said, "get me a useful way to make a living, make a difference."

"Doing what?"

"Emptying bedpans in a nursing home or dishwashing at the homeless shelter. I keep thinking about stuff. The ghosts follow me, watch what I do. Actually, they're becoming good company."

"Let them stay," Ellie said. "Everyone needs company. Just don't talk to them in public."

He threw his head back and howled. "I think they have their own grief and I'm just part of it. We share."

"Yeah. Probably," she said. "Grief doesn't go away. It scabs over. Leaves a scar."

"Yeah, a scar. Sometimes more than one."

He stood, offered a hand down, pulled her to standing, wrapped his arms around her while he nuzzled her neck and nibbled at her ear. She snuggled into their intertwined arms, shared warmth, and held on tight. They stood and swayed slightly, moving together.

Morning colors changed from milk to pale tangerine. An early beachcomber glided past, intent on exposed high-tide treasures. The sun climbed toward the horizon and glared down at the creatures scurrying before the promised day. A brown pelican floated overhead then dove for fish beneath the surface. Small terns, forked tails trembling, hovered over sea swells before diving.

"Can you ever forgive yourself?" she said.

"I don't know. Maybe. Can you forgive yourself?"

"I don't know either. Everything takes time."

They sat silent until it was full light.

Still silent, they gathered the quilt, shook the loose sand off, and crossed the dunes to the car. The empty bottles clinked against each other, a percussive refrain accompanying the gull acrobatics and swish of white caps.

The *áo dài* clad woman melted into the haze.

Chapter 59
Departure

September 1970

Reid slept restless. Sleep-defeated, he got up and dressed, made coffee, and sat outside on the stoop drinking a cup. Not quite light, songbirds twittered as nocturnal beings relinquished their hold and surrendered to day creatures. Bugle lay with head on her paws and watched his face, occasionally shifting or thumping her tail. A cat waltzed across the yard intent on feline comings and goings.

Thin shards of light had barely crossed the sky when Angela stepped outside. She and Reid sat in peaceful silence. Gathering clouds promised rain after the last parched summer weeks. The oaks began their fall job of shedding leaves. The scent of figs rotting on the ground and dust drifted across the yard.

Reid finished his coffee and tossed the sediments beside the steps. Angela held out her hand for the cup. He gave it to her, then rose and kissed the top of her head.

"My stuff's already in the car. Take care of Bugle and the cats. Be sure that old mule and Pansy stay together." He squeezed her shoulder and stepped off the stoop toward the Corvair.

Halfway to the car, he stopped, put his hands in his

pockets, and craned his head up to look at the translucent sky. His voice came back toward her thick, cracks flitting along the edges.

"I love you, Sis."

"I love you too, little brother. Remember where you came from."

Chapter 60
Mid-Day

September 1970

The voice had a muted quality, sharp charcoal edges ground smooth. *We have to go. You and me. They're waiting for us. All of them are out there waiting.*

Reid settled into the car seat, pushed the lighter in, and touched it briefly to the tip of his cigarette. He pulled deep on the roll-up, his cheeks hollow, and recognized the nicotine coursing through his thoughts.

The engine coughed several times, caught, and loped unsteadily as he maneuvered the vehicle south by slightly southwest.

Black clad figures sat on the car hood, the wind blowing their mourning headbands. They pointed an ancient rifle at an image clad in camouflage standing beside the road. The figure did not flinch from the rifle but dissolved into the day as the car sped past.

"We can see the boys again," Reid said.

Yes. See the boys again. Even the greenies.

"Yes."

Alone. Everyone's alone.

"No. We're all connected," Reid said. "I had to come back for Ellie and Angela. But there's no return home. Things are different, changed."

Truth changes with time.

"Yes. Time will make a difference."

Reid stubbed his cigarette out in the ash tray, smiled to himself, and accelerated.

Chapter 61
Feelings, Memories

October 1970

Weeks later, Ellie sat on her porch swing, drank coffee, and watched rain rivulets wash the azalea bushes and saturate the weeds. Grover sat nearby and sniffed the air. Rosie minced along the banister, jumped onto the swing, and purring, curled into Ellie's lap.

The downpour moved like the summer squall that had soaked Ellie and Reid's beginning, years ago, mirroring their ache and fever. Fat drops bathed the backyard picnic table and settled into the carved indentions—April 1965.

Only a month previously, he had driven away from the farm and out of South Carolina, leaving scraps and pieces of himself behind. Her memory of him fragile, like a dream, appeared and disappeared, and changed and changed again.

When he first shipped, she held on to the love and angst he had left behind. She mulled over the loss of their baby and her own years of waiting. She understood past things: Angela's grace and grit, both before and after Jim Guy's death, the cost of the Old Man's life and his hard passing, and the significance of Reid's farm years. She recognized the door Diana had flung open revealing unexplored inner layers. Another woman, a world away, closed her door. Ghosts lingered. Each brought warts and beauty to their checkered mix.

Down the street, moss ropes dangled heavy and wet from ancient oaks. The paperboy, poncho flapping, peddled through a puddle and tossed her newspaper on the porch. She waved a thank you.

Four months afterward, Ellie opened the mailbox and pulled out a stack of bills, sale flyers, and junk mail. She fingered a postcard with Mile-Marker 0 on the front, stroked the glossy picture, and flipped it over for the printed caption:

Only 2,377 miles from Fort Kent, Maine to Key West, Florida.

Below the caption, a single line was scrawled on the back, no signature:

Ellie,
They say Cuba offers the best in rum and deep-sea fishing. I'll let you know.

Reid's brooding voice, his chicken-scratch writing, underlying thoughtfulness, and terrible guilt hovered between the lines. She saw again his crooked smile and scarred hand. At least, he called her Ellie, not Eleanor.

At times, she had harbored a howling, predatory love for him. Memories of sweaty nights, belly-deep laughter, and days lost to the morass of Vietnam shattered her heart, left jagged shards. Now, with the sharp edges dulled, some things were the same, and other things irrevocably different. She savored the past, understood its comforts.

Closing the mailbox, she clomped up the wooden porch steps and sat in the swing. Grover put his head in her knee.

"Home is a place in the mind," she said aloud. "Besides, those that wait, also serve. That's me. And you." She ruffled Grover's ears. He thumped his tail in response.

She tucked the card in her shirt pocket and stroked her bulging belly. Twice now Reid had left her alone and pregnant. Looking back, she struggled to remember what she had shared with him. Love. Tenderness, sometimes. And relief.

Chapter 62
Postcards

July 1972

Every few months, an unsigned postcard arrives. Ellie and Angela get together, eat pistachio ice cream, and read the card. They hover over the postal mark, look for the town on a map, and speculate about Reid's location. Sometimes, they vary the ice cream.

Nine months after Reid left, Ellie delivered their baby Joy Linh Holcombe. Joy for the happiness she brings and Linh for the other woman in her father's life.

Reid moves frequently, so Ellie's uncertain if he realizes he has a daughter. She thinks the ghosts still keep him company.

One year into her master's program, she continues working with the Chamber and the Gullah-Geechee Project. The income's solid and the research is the core of her graduate degree.

Angela teaches, cares for her market garden, and paints. She takes pleasure in being Joy's auntie.

Occasionally, late of a summer afternoon, Ellie drives to the coastal islands with Grover, his head out the window and ears flapping. She relaxes into the seat, savors the salt air, and the blowing wind. It's the same road she and Reid drove together all those years ago.

She drives. And remembers.

A word about the author...

Nancy Hartney writes nonfiction and short stories. *Washed in Water: Tales from the South*, her debut collection of short stories, was chosen Best Fiction of the Year 2014 by Ozark Writers League. Her second collection, *If the Creek Don't Rise*, continues to receive critical acclaim.

Her short stories and poetry have been published in literary journals and her western tales in regional collections.

She contributes to various magazines and newsletters with articles on foxhunting, rodeo, horse events, and mule jumping. Non-fiction, general interest, and other work appears in area publications and historical quarterlies.

A member of the writing community, she works with the Ozark Writers League (MO), Ozark Creative Writers (AR), Tallahassee Writers Association (FL), Oklahoma Writers Federation, Inc., and area libraries, often leading workshops, book discussion groups, and judging short story contests.

Find her at NancyHartney.com

Thank you for purchasing
this publication of The Wild Rose Press, Inc.

For questions or more information
contact us at
info@thewildrosepress.com.

The Wild Rose Press, Inc.
www.thewildrosepress.com

CPSIA information can be obtained
at www.ICGtesting.com
Printed in the USA
LVHW051628090221
678835LV00011B/1236